Travis's hands rested loosely on her waist.
LaRaine slid her fingers into the curling black
hair at his neck to force his head down. The
touch of his hard lips on hers was warm
and undemanding.

The initiative had been hers but now Travis
was taking over. His mouth continued its
exploration of hers, the firm pressure subtly
teasing. There was a fluttering weakness in her
stomach. For the first time in her life LaRaine
wanted to respond naturally to a man's kiss.
Then he was slowly lifting his head and
unwinding her arms from around his neck.

"Are you bored, LaRaine?" His voice taunted
her. "Are you seeking a diversion, an affair
with a local cowboy to pass the time?"

JANET DAILEY AMERICANA

ALABAMA—Dangerous Masquerade
ALASKA—Northern Magic
ARIZONA—Sonora Sundown
ARKANSAS—Valley of the Vapours
CALIFORNIA—Fire and Ice
COLORADO—After the Storm
CONNECTICUT—Difficult Decision
DELAWARE—The Matchmakers
FLORIDA—Southern Nights
GEORGIA—Night of the Cotillion
HAWAII—Kona Winds
IDAHO—The Travelling Kind
ILLINOIS—A Lyon's Share
INDIANA—The Indy Man
IOWA—The Homeplace
KANSAS—The Mating Season
KENTUCKY—Bluegrass King
LOUISIANA—The Bride of the Delta Queen
MAINE—Summer Mahogany
MARYLAND—Bed of Grass
MASSACHUSETTS—That Boston Man
MICHIGAN—Enemy in Camp
MINNESOTA—Giant of Mesabi
MISSISSIPPI—A Tradition of Pride
MISSOURI—Show Me

MONTANA—Big Sky Country
NEBRASKA—Boss Man from Ogallala
NEVADA—Reilly's Woman
NEW HAMPSHIRE—Heart of Stone
NEW JERSEY—One of the Boys
NEW MEXICO—Land of Enchantment
NEW YORK—Beware of the Stranger
NORTH CAROLINA—That Carolina Summer
NORTH DAKOTA—Lord of the High Lonesome
OHIO—The Widow and the Wastrel
OKLAHOMA—Six White Horses
OREGON—To Tell the Truth
PENNSYLVANIA—The Thawing of Mara
RHODE ISLAND—Strange Bedfellow
SOUTH CAROLINA—Low Country Liar
SOUTH DAKOTA—Dakota Dreamin'
TENNESSEE—Sentimental Journey
TEXAS—Savage Land
UTAH—A Land Called Deseret
VERMONT—Green Mountain Man
VIRGINIA—Tide Water Lover
WASHINGTON—For Mike's Sake
WEST VIRGINIA—Wild and Wonderful
WISCONSIN—With a Little Luck
WYOMING—Darling Jenny

Janet Dailey
Americana

A LAND CALLED DESERET

Harlequin Books

TORONTO • NEW YORK • LONDON
AMSTERDAM • PARIS • SYDNEY • HAMBURG
STOCKHOLM • ATHENS • TOKYO • MILAN
MADRID • WARSAW • BUDAPEST • AUCKLAND

The state flower depicted on the cover of this book is sego lily.

Janet Dailey Americana edition published March 1988
Second printing October 1988
Third printing October 1989
Fourth printing October 1990
Fifth printing December 1991
Sixth printing September 1992
Seventh printing November 1992

ISBN 0-373-89894-0

Harlequin Presents edition published December 1979
Second printing February 1982

Original hardcover edition published in 1979
by Mills & Boon Limited

A LAND CALLED DESERET

CHAPTER ONE

A HOT WIND blew dust through the opened windows of the four-wheel drive Scout, coating everything in sight with a red brown film. The fine grit clogged the pores of LaRaine's skin, particles clinging to the gloss on her lips until she could taste it in her mouth. She couldn't breathe without the dust filtering into her lungs. The dry, dusty smell of it overpowered the scent of the expensive perfume she wore.

Through the amber shade of her sunglasses, her dark eyes smarted from the dust and could see no relief ahead. The raw, harsh land stretching around her was marked with jutting mesas and slashing arroyos. Yellow grass dug tenacious roots into the inhospitable earth while stubby, gnarled trees offered questionable shade.

The Scout bounced over the rutted track that passed for a road. Above the roar of the engine could be heard the groaning, thumping rattle of protest it made. LaRaine clutched the armrest of the passenger door to keep from bouncing all over the seat, the scarlet sheen of her long fingernails contrasting vividly with the beige upholstery.

"I'm surprised somebody hasn't given Utah back to the Indians," she muttered.

The man driving darted a glance at his raven-haired passenger. His attention couldn't be spared for long from the road as the ruts tried to wrench the steering wheel from his hands. Sam Hardesty saw LaRaine wipe her throat and neck with a handkerchief and saw her grimace at the grimy dirt that perspiration had gathered. The mirrorlike finish of his sunglasses hid the glitter of amusement that danced in his eyes.

A gust of wind sent a choking cloud of dust into the interior of the four-wheel-drive vehicle. LaRaine coughed and covered her mouth with one hand while the other waved the handkerchief as if to clear the air.

"How much farther do we have to go?" she demanded, her voice choked with dust and tested patience.

"McCrea's ranch can't be far now." Sam Hardesty successfully hid a smile at LaRaine's obvious discomfort.

"That's what you said twenty minutes ago." She coughed again and futilely wagged the handkerchief in front of her. "I'm going to choke to death on this dust before we get there!"

"Roll the window up if it's getting to be too much for you," he suggested without sympathy.

"Excellent idea, Sam," she agreed sarcastically. "With the window up, this rattletrap excuse for a car turns into a furnace."

"You asked to come with me," he reminded her. "Nobody twisted your arm."

"I never dreamed it would be like this. I thought you'd take one of the limousines, or, at the very least, one of the cars that was air-conditioned. Instead you take this." There was no mistaking the contempt in her voice for their mode of transportation. Her slashing glance to the driver caught the silent twitch of laughter at the corners of his mouth. "And stop smirking! It isn't the least bit funny."

"Can you imagine any of the cars from the studio traveling over this?" He gestured briefly to the rough road ahead of them before grabbing the wheel with both hands again. "Springs, shocks—the whole bottom of those cars would be torn out before they could get a mile. Besides, you could have changed your mind when you saw I was taking the Scout."

"I wish I had," she insisted tightly.

"No, you don't." Amusement colored his dismissal of her statement. "When you found out about Mc-Crea, you would have walked to get to his place. The minute you heard the words 'local rancher,' all your antennae came out. Is he single? Is he rich? Is he handsome? When the feedback was positive, you decided then and there to be the first member of the cast to meet him. You intend to establish your claim on him before anyone else finds out he's around."

It was on the tip of LaRaine's tongue to deny his allegation, but Sam knew her too well. She would never be able to convince him that she was just along for the ride. His words did wound, though. He made her sound so mercenary, but in a sense, she supposed she was.

"I wouldn't care if McCrea were fat, bald and eighty," she stated to boldly deny that she felt a sense of guilt at her motives. "Any diversion would be welcome in this godforsaken hole of the world!"

"I think you're being sensible." Sam briefly met her look of surprise. "I'm serious. You need to find yourself a rich husband because you don't have any future as an actress. The only part you can get is when you play yourself. There aren't that many roles that call for a greedy, grasping bitch."

LaRaine paled at his stabbing jibe, but she doubted that her dust-coated face revealed it. She had become an expert at concealing her true feelings, such an expert that she sometimes wondered if she felt anything anymore.

"Your bitterness is showing, Sam," she replied coldly, and stared sightlessly out of the window. "I didn't realize it still bothered you that I turned down your marriage proposal. As a struggling young assistant producer, you can't afford me."

"I was a fool to think I could, wasn't I?" Sam's response was sardonically dry as he pushed a wisp of thin brown hair from his forehead. "But, like a lot of others, I was blinded by your beauty. I didn't realize until it was too late that you were only using me to make sure you landed this part in the film."

"I needed the role." Financially and in every other way, her career had been spiralling downward rapidly. "And I'm grateful for all the support you gave me."

"Your thanks are very empty." His mouth was grim as he shifted the vehicle into a lower gear.

"Did you expect payment for your help? Maybe you thought I'd go to bed with you?" Her volatile temper flared. "I may be guilty of a lot of things, but using the casting couch isn't one of them!"

"No, you just dangle suckers like me until you get

what you want, then you cut the line," Sam muttered. "The word is spreading. You aren't going to find many more suckers you can hook. You were a fool, LaRaine, to ever let Montgomery slip out of your fingers."

"I dropped him," she lied.

"And he fell right into your cousin's hands, didn't he?" taunted Sam.

"She's welcome to him," LaRaine insisted with a trace of hauteur. The vehicle bounced in and out of a pothole and she narrowly missed hitting her head on the ceiling. The rough ride was bruising. "I hope it'll all be worth it when we reach the ranch," she murmured the thought aloud.

"It will be worth it, believe me," was the faintly smug reply.

But her thoughts were already refocusing on a previous comment from Sam. Rian Montgomery had possessed all the attributes she had sought in a husband, a wealthy, powerful figure with ruthless good looks. The mere fact that she had attracted his attention and had worn his engagement ring was the reason she had been offered her first supporting role in a movie.

Foolishly she had grabbed at the part, confident of her ability to maneuver Rian Montgomery. LaRaine had never believed for a minute that he loved her, or that she loved him. They had suited each other's purpose. He had wanted an ornamental wife to entertain his business associates and maintain a beautiful home, someone who would make no demands on him and who would be satisfied with presents instead of affection.

That type of arrangement had satisfied LaRaine until

she had been offered that part in a movie. She had seen
the chance to obtain glamor and fame in her own
right, so she took it. She had the looks and the figure.
By the time she had discovered she didn't have the
talent to be a success, Rian had learned about her
deception in accepting the initial role and concealing it
from him. He had broken their engagement and married her cousin.

LaRaine's mother, who had raised both LaRaine and
her cousin Laurie, had accused Laurie of stealing Rian
from her daughter, but LaRaine didn't blame her.
Many times she had envied her cousin during their early
years. Neither of her parents had expected Laurie to
excel in anything, but they had practically demanded
that LaRaine be the best at everything—having the
highest grades, the best clothes and being the prettiest
girl, the most sought-after girl friend, the most popular
one in her class.

Since that first movie and the broken engagement
to Rian, LaRaine had managed to obtain a handful
of other roles, each one smaller than the last. A
half-dozen marriage proposals had been made to her,
but all had come from men whose prospects for the
future looked no brighter than her own. LaRaine's upbringing had forced her to believe she deserved the
best. It was too deeply ingrained for her to settle for
less.

Some, and Sam Hardesty was among them, had accused her of being too deeply in love with herself to
love anyone else. It wasn't true. If the accusations
hadn't hurt so much, they would have been funny. She
had become classified as a cold, calculating woman,

and she had begun to act the part with more finesse than she had ever displayed on the screen.

This movie being filmed on location in Utah would probably be her last job in the industry. The critics were crucifying her acting in her most recently released movie with Jim Corbett. She hadn't a prayer of being hired again.

The thought of James Corbett brought a painful, self-deprecating smile to her scarlet red lips. She had so stupidly believed that she had a chance of catching him. She had even imagined declaring to the world that she was giving up her acting career for him—when in truth there had been no career to give up.

LaRaine was desperate. Her parents, especially her mother, were angry with her because she didn't fight to take Rian Montgomery away from her cousin and upset because she was doing so poorly in her career. She had no friends. A marriage seemed to be the only way she could save face. But it had to be someone outside Hollywood, someone who wouldn't know of her reputation or her humiliating put-downs by Rian Montgomery and Jim Corbett. Who better to dazzle with her status as an actress than a wealthy Utah rancher? At least, that was LaRaine's fervent hope.

The four-wheel-drive vehicle bounced over a ridge and rolled to a stop. LaRaine glanced around, looking for some indication that they had reached their destination. There wasn't a building in sight, only more vast stretches of wasteland. She hadn't expected the country to be so desolate, which was how it seemed to her.

"Carl was right," Sam mused aloud. "This will be an excellent backdrop for those ranch sequences."

"This?" LaRaine looked around once again, unable to see it through his eyes. "But there's nothing here."

"Precisely." He started the Scout forward.

A wheel briefly spun into the dust, sending a gritty cloud through the open window. LaRaine coughed. "How much farther?"

"Just over the rise. You can see the roofs of the buildings." Sam pointed, a half-smile curving his mouth.

"Thank God," LaRaine murmured. She opened her bag and took out a hand mirror. "I look a mess!"

The wind had played havoc with the curling black curtain of her hair, rumpling it into provocative disorder. Dabbing at the perspiration streaks, she took care not to ruin the makeup that highlighted her striking bone structure.

"I wouldn't worry, LaRaine," Sam observed. "You're the only woman I know who can look stunning when she's a mess."

LaRaine wasn't sure if he meant that. "Thanks," she returned, but her voice was as dry as her throat. She added a fresh touch of vivid red lipgloss and decided that was the best she could do under the circumstances.

As the vehicle crested the rise, her anticipation soared. She had expected to see a modern, sprawling ranch house complete with stable and barn and immaculate white-fenced corrals, and her brown eyes widened in shock at the ranch buildings before them.

The massive house was an old, two-story affair. The hot sun had long ago blistered the paint from the boards. The flat gray color added years to the structure's age. Both the barn and a small shed seemed on the verge of falling down, their siding equally bereft of paint. A late model pickup truck was parked near the shed, its color hidden by the thick coating of dust.

The single corral was constructed out of leftover posts, boards and logs, a conglomeration of materials that made it appear less substantial than it was. A windmill creaked noisily in the gusting wind, adding to the feeling of total dilapidation.

"Surprised?" Sam's voice mocked her expression as he stopped the Scout in front of the house.

LaRaine removed her sunglasses to turn her dark, accusing eyes on him. "You knew it was going to look like this, didn't you?"

"Carl gave me a pretty good description of the place," he admitted.

"And you led me to believe this rancher had money!" Frustration throbbed in her voice, mixing with anger.

"I never said he had money." Sam opened his door and stepped out. "I said he was well-to-do. Like most ranchers, McCrea is rich in land and cattle, but poor in money. Why else would he be willing to sell us permission to film on his land? He needs the cash."

Pushing open her door, LaRaine stepped out. She brushed at the dust that powdered the ivory silk of her blouse; the action sent puffs of dust in the air. A closer look at the buildings didn't improve their appearance.

"I hope you're planning to offer him enough money so that he can afford to buy some paint," she declared, disappointment tasting bitter.

"I'm sure there'll be enough," Sam answered, but his thoughts were elsewhere. Behind the sunglasses, his gaze had narrowed to inspect the premises. "This place could be used to film the nesters scene. I'll have to make sure he doesn't paint anything until we decide."

"That arrogance is typical of you producers. You give a man money, then tell him when he can spend it," she retorted with biting softness.

Sam merely smiled and walked to the porch. La-Raine didn't follow; she doubted that the porch floor would hold the weight of two people. She waited beside the Scout, wiping at the dust on the soft fawn leather of her split riding skirt. The screen door rattled when Sam knocked on it. The swirling wind billowed the light blue windbreaker that protected his slender torso. He knocked again.

"Doesn't seem to be anyone home," he decided, and walked off the porch. A chicken scratched the dirt in his path and clucked in protest as it was forced to move out of his way.

"Did you tell him that you were coming by this morning?" LaRaine wondered aloud. "Or did you just expect him to be here when you showed up?"

"No, that's something you would do," Sam retorted. "You always expect people to be around when you want them. I called McCrea last night to tell him I'd be by this morning." He pushed back the elastic cuff of his windbreaker to look at his wristwatch. "Carl warned me about the road, so I told McCrea not to expect me until around eleven. It's a couple of minutes before that now."

His passing remark that she expected people at her beck and call had hurt, and LaRaine tried to get back at him. "I'd laugh if he's changed his mind about letting you film on his land."

"You wouldn't laugh for long," he told her as he walked around to the driver's side. "Any more delays would mean budget cuts. Your role isn't all that essential. You might remember that, LaRaine."

"Are you threatening me, Sam?" For all the laughing challenge in her voice, LaRaine was inwardly intimidated by his statement. "I didn't realize what a sore loser you were, that you'd contemplate revenge."

"Revenge might be sweet," was the only response he made as he reached inside the opened window of the vehicle to honk the horn.

The blaring sound sent the chickens scurrying, wings flapping, to the rear of the house. LaRaine felt sick and frightened, but she wouldn't let Sam see that. Her downcast gaze glimpsed the dust on her knee-high boots. The handkerchief had been used to wipe everything else; she decided she might as well use it on her leather boots.

Resting a toe on the chrome bumper, she bent to wipe away the dust from her boot. A swipe of the linen cloth brought out the high-polished sheen of the fine leather, a darker, complementing shade of brown to the riding skirt she wore. With one boot free of dust, she shifted her attention to the other.

"That must be McCrea coming now," Sam announced.

LaRaine glanced up to see a horse and rider approaching the ranchyard. She held her pose, one foot on the front bumper of the vehicle and an elbow resting casually on a raised knee. Her attitude of indifferent interest was feigned as she studied the horse and rider coming toward them.

The muscled conformation of the mahogany bay horse was flawless. LaRaine was a novice when it came to ranches and cattle, but she did know good horseflesh, and the horse the man was riding was no ordinary nag. As they came closer, LaRaine realized that the horse was not only powerfully muscled, but tall as well, standing easily sixteen hands high. Its running walk ate up the ground with effortless ease.

When she got a better look at the rider, she saw that the horse had to be big in order to carry the man on its back. Anything smaller than the bay and the rider would have dwarfed his mount, making a combination as incongruous as an adult on a Shetland pony.

The man was big, tall with a broad chest and shoulders. Despite his size, he rode with effortless grace, relaxed and at ease as if born in the saddle. LaRaine could see little of his face beneath the brim of his sweat-stained cowboy hat. What was visible was mostly strong jaw and chin.

Saddle leather creaked as the horse and rider entered the ranchyard. A red calf was draped across the saddle in front of the rider. It hung limp, showing no sign of life, when the horse was reined to a stop in front of the barn.

Gathering the calf in his arms, the rider stepped down from the saddle. As yet, the man had not acknowledged their presence with more than a look. Sam walked forward to meet him, but LaRaine waited.

"Hi, I'm Sam Hardesty from the movie studio." He introduced himself, not bothering to extend a hand since the rancher's arms were holding the calf. "I called you last night."

The calf wasn't as small as it had first appeared. LaRaine guessed that it easily weighed over a hundred pounds, but the rancher carried its limp weight with ease.

"Sorry I wasn't here when you arrived, Mr. Hardesty." The man's voice was pitched low, with a pleasant drawl despite the business tone. "Do you mind if we hold off our talk for a few minutes? This calf is in bad shape. I have to tend to him first."

"I don't mind a bit," Sam replied with the faintest trace of impatience creeping into his answer.

LaRaine removed her boot from the bumper and moved a couple of steps to bring her in line with the path the man was taking to the house. She tipped her head at a provocative angle, letting the black cloud of her hair drift to one side.

"Was I deceived or did I detect a trace of Texas in your voice?" she questioned in a deliberately playful challenge.

The man stopped. A pair of brown eyes inspected LaRaine with almost insulting indifference to her feminine beauty. Meeting him face to face, she noticed the wings of gray in his otherwise dark hair. Even though he carried the calf, she could tell that the broad shoulders tapered to a slim waist and hips, giving a deceptive impression of leanness. And it was deceptive. Her petite frame was dwarfed by his bulk.

"Yes, I'm from Texas originally," he admitted, and turned his brown eyes on Sam.

The look prompted an introduction. "Mr. McCrea,

this is one of the supporting actresses in our film, Miss LaRaine Evans. She came along to get an idea of the lie of the land." His sly innuendo wasn't wasted on La-Raine. Sam had meant that she was checking the rancher out.

She had the suspicion that the rancher knew exactly what Sam meant. It was an unnerving feeling. She had expected him to be something of a country bumpkin, unversed in the subtleties of life, someone who could easily be tricked. She caught a hint of worldly sophistication in those glittering brown eyes, despite the obvious brute force.

"LaRaine, this is Travis McCrea," Sam finished the introduction.

"It's a pleasure, Miss Evans," the rancher offered in greeting.

"Please, call me LaRaine," she insisted with a wide smile.

"Thank you." His head dipped in acknowledgment, the hat brim concealing the glitter of mockery she briefly glimpsed in his eyes. "Excuse me, I have to take care of the calf."

Travis McCrea moved past her onto the porch, which surprisingly supported the combined weight of the rancher and the calf. It didn't sit well with LaRaine that this man found her subtle flirtation amusing. He had been impressed by neither her looks nor the fact that she was an actress, two things she had been counting on. She had struck out, and Sam was finding that laughable.

As she started to follow the two men into the house, her gaze swept the weathered boards of the house. The appearance of the house didn't match its owner. Her previous disappointment in the surroundings had faded when she had seen Travis McCrea for the first time. He didn't strike her as the kind of man who would be content to live in this hovel. So why was he?

It was a puzzle and one she couldn't solve until she had more answers to the questions buzzing in her head. Sam was holding the screen door open for her. LaRaine put a tentative boot on the porch floorboards. They were more solid than they appeared and she walked forward. The interior of the house might be totally different from the outside. Then the thought crossed her mind—how different could it be if Travis McCrea was taking a calf inside?

CHAPTER TWO

THE PORCH DOOR opened into the living room. In La-
Raine's estimation, it was furnished with Salvation Army rejects. A couch and chair were covered in a hideous
maroon with a thin gold stripe. An overstuffed recliner
in cheap vinyl leather was in front of a smoke-blackened
fireplace. An area rug covered the linoleum floor. La-
Raine guessed that the rug might have once possessed an
Oriental pattern, but it was so threadbare, the color and
design had faded into meaningless combinations.

There were water stains on the ceilings in both the
living room and the hallway leading into the kitchen.
Both areas had the same wallpaper, equally yellowed
with age and with seams curling away from the wall.
The few pictures that had been on the wall resembled
old calendar covers that had been framed. LaRaine
looked around with disdain. If it were possible, the interior of the house was worse than the outside.

A darkened staircase branched off the hallway to the
second floor. LaRaine shuddered at what might be in
the rooms above. She followed the men's voices into
the kitchen. There, the linoleum floor had cracked in
several places, exposing black seams splintering across
a scuffed, yellow-splattered pattern. The wood cabinets
were finished in a cherry-wood stain.

Gray tile rose halfway up the walls where a band of brick-patterned wallpaper separated the tile from the upper half of the wall painted a sickly shade of green. The wooden table in the center of the room looked as if it had fifteen coats of brown paint on it. The surrounding chairs were all in different styles, from an armed captain's chair to a severe straight-backed chair.

Everything about the house made LaRaine want to cringe. The only thing that could be said in its favor was that it was clean. Even that couldn't make up for the deplorable lack of taste used in decorating it.

The red calf had been laid on a braided throw rug in a cleared area of the room. Travis McCrea was kneeling at its head while Sam hovered nearby, watching. LaRaine's intense dislike for the house didn't extend to its owner. She walked around the ugly brown table to stand near them.

"What happened to the calf?" she asked to make conversation.

"He got a faceful and noseful of thorns," was Travis's response as he continued working near the calf's head without glancing up. "He either tangled with some cactus or a patch of briars."

Travis moved and LaRaine noticed the tweezerlike instrument in his hand and glimpsed the swollen and festering sores around the calf's nose and eyes. It was a repelling sight, but she forced herself to remain indifferent.

"How did it happen?" She found it difficult to believe that even a dumb animal could have something like that happen to it.

"I wouldn't even begin to guess." Travis shrugged to

indicate the "how" was immaterial at this point. "Maybe something frightened it into stampeding into the thorns."

Although LaRaine didn't have a clear view, she could tell that he was pulling out some of the thorns and cutting out others that had worked themselves in too deep. Despite the obvious pain Travis had to be inflicting, the calf didn't make a sound or struggle.

"Is it alive?" She was beginning to doubt it. She glanced at its rib cage to see if she could tell whether or not it was breathing. The movement was very faint.

"He's alive, but just barely. It must have happened a couple of days ago or more," Travis explained. "He hasn't been able to eat, maybe not even able to drink, since then. He's very weak."

"Will he live?" It was Sam who put forward the question.

"I don't know." The grim mouth quirked briefly. "I'll tell you in a couple of days." Raising his head, Travis cast a glance sideways at LaRaine. "There's antiseptic and some swabs in the cabinet by the back door. Would you get them for me?"

She hesitated for a fraction of a second, then walked to the cupboard he had indicated. The bottle of antiseptic and swabs were exactly where he had said they were. She carried them to where he knelt beside the calf.

"Is the calf worth saving?" Sam questioned.

"He's worth saving, if for nothing else, than to butcher as beef for my own use." A note of dryness crept into Travis's otherwise patient voice. With a nod of his head, he indicated that LaRaine should kneel beside him. When she did, she was made aware again of how powerfully muscled his shoulders and arms were. One of his hands was equal to almost both of hers. Amidst the animal smells clinging to him, she caught the tang of his after-shave lotion. "Your hands are cleaner than mine. You apply the antiseptic and I'll hold the calf's head still."

LaRaine stared at the swollen, and now bloodied, face of the injured calf, stunned by the request Travis had made. So many of the wounds were close to the eyes, nose and mouth. She had heard or read somewhere that antiseptic could be fatal if swallowed. She had never treated a sick thing in her life, and the thought kept running through her mind that she could accidently kill it in her ignorance.

"I...I can't," she stammered out her stunned refusal, shoving the bottle toward him and recoiling.

"It's very simple. You just—" Travis began to explain with taut patience.

"Save it," Sam interrupted, his voice laced with scorn. "I'm sure LaRaine doesn't want to risk staining her leather skirt with the medicine. Ornamental, the lovely lady is, but useful she definitely isn't."

There was a suggestion of contempt in the dismissing glance Travis gave her. "My mistake. I should have realized you wouldn't want to risk soiling your clothes." He placed the faintest emphasis on the pronoun "you." "Move to the side." It was an order, not a request. It all happened so quickly that LaRaine didn't have a chance to refute Sam's statement. "Would you mind holding the calf's head, Mr. Hardesty? He's been pretty quiet up until now, but I don't want to take any chances."

"Be glad to help. What do you want me to do?" Sam moved closer while LaRaine shifted out of the way and rose to her feet.

She watched as Travis showed Sam what he wanted. She could have done that, but she hadn't been asked. LaRaine kept silent. Why on earth should she regret not being able to treat an animal? It was stupid and silly. She should be glad she didn't have to touch that smelly, infected creature.

"In the same cupboard where you found the antiseptic, there's a black container with a syringe inside," Travis told her. "Would you get that for me, and the vial of antibiotics in the refrigerator?"

The syringe LaRaine located right away, but she had to look for the vial in the refrigerator. She brought both of them to Travis as he finished disinfecting the wounds. Sam looked away as Travis jabbed the needle into the calf. LaRaine had never been squeamish about such things as shots or the sight of blood. She had watched all the rancher's ministrations to the calf with a kind of curious fascination.

"You can let go of him," Travis told Sam.

The calf weakly kicked out with a hind leg when Sam relaxed his hold and straightened to his feet. It seemed to be breathing more easily. LaRaine wondered if the swelling had affected its nasal passages. Poor little thing, it looked so helpless lying there on the rug. She resisted the impulse to kneel beside it and pet its tangled red hide. Sam would only make fun of her and silently accuse her of doing it to impress Travis McCrea. Instead, she hooked her thumbs in the waistband of her riding skirt, pretending an indifference to the plight of the calf.

"What will you do with the calf now?" she asked. "You aren't going to turn it loose, are you?"

"Right now I'm going to mix up some mash and calf milk to see if I can get some nourishment down him. Then I'll put him in one of the stalls in the barn until he's up and around again before I turn him loose." Behind the surface blandness of the strongly defined male features, LaRaine had the impression that Travis was mockingly inquiring whether or not his plan met with her approval.

It irritated her. "I see." She looked away, aware that there were dark sparks shooting in her eyes. "Tell me, do you always treat your sick animals in the kitchen?" The audacious demand slipped out before she could get control of her irritation.

"Not all the time. Some of the animals I can't get through the door. In this case, it seemed easier to bring the calf to the equipment than to bring the equipment and medicine to the calf. I didn't realize that you would object if I treated *my* animals in *my* kitchen." He stressed the possessive pronoun with challenging emphasis.

LaRaine turned away, aware that she had put her foot in her mouth again. "Of course I don't object. I was merely curious."

"And I always thought curiosity killed the cat," Sam murmured, and LaRaine wanted to hiss at him like a cat after that remark.

Instead she responded with frigid control. "Doesn't

the rest of the verse say something about satisfaction bringing it back?" But she couldn't resist one playful claw at her former boyfriend. "You mustn't pay any attention to Sam, Mr. McCrea. He's bitter because he asked me to marry him and I turned him down." She watched Sam turn red with anger and gave him a tiny feline smile.

Sam grabbed her arm and half turned her so that her back was to Travis, who seemed to find the interplay between them beneath his attention. LaRaine didn't like being ignored any more than she liked being the butt of some secret joke.

"Dammit, LaRaine," Sam muttered beneath his breath. "This is a business meeting between myself and McCrea. I said you could come along, but I'm not going to let you start dragging personalities into the conversation."

"You started it, darling." She ran her fingernails lightly across his shaven cheek in a mock scratch, then disdainfully twisted her arm free of his hold. In a louder voice, addressed to both men, she said, "Since you have business to discuss, I think I'll get some fresh air."

Neither man made a single protest as she walked from the kitchen. LaRaine was in one of those moods where even that angered her. Out of sheer politeness they could have pretended that she was welcome to stay.

In a burst of temper, she let the screen door slam loudly shut. Walking off the porch, she kicked at a rock. It bounced over the ground and sent a chicken squawking for cover. The bay horse stood in front of the barn, the ends of the reins dragging the ground. Under other circumstances, LaRaine might have wandered over to it. It wasn't her horse, so why should she care if it was still saddled and standing in the sun?

Nothing had gone the way she planned it. The ride here had been a miserable, bone-jarring, bruising experience. The ranch was a despicable place and Travis McCrea had not fallen at her feet, figuratively or literally, when he'd met her. She felt close to tears, which was ridiculous. She never cried. She stared at the distant horizon and blinked at the smarting moistness.

The screen door opened, the sound followed by heavy footsteps on the porch floorboards. LaRaine didn't turn around. There were two sets of feet, Sam's and Travis McCrea's.

"That business discussion was short but sweet," LaRaine said, to let them know she was aware they had joined her outside.

"It isn't over." It was Travis who responded to her comment. "I came out to bed the calf down in one of the stalls."

"Oh." Her reply was an indifferent sound as she pretended that she didn't care what either of them did.

Out of the corner of her eye, she could see Travis's bulk only a few feet away. The calf was in his arms. This time it was making an attempt to hold its head up, the purple splotches of antiseptic on its white face.

"Are you admiring the view?" Travis asked.

"Yes." LaRaine agreed rather than turn to look at him. She was afraid that the brightness of unshed tears might be in her eyes and she didn't want him to see. A further comment seemed to be expected from her and she searched for one. "It's a vast, beautiful. . . ." The lie stuck in her throat. She couldn't find anything beautiful about the desolate country. "Nothing," she finished with cold, blatant truthfulness.

"Yes." Travis seemed to consider her reply. "You could be right."

LaRaine felt his gaze dwelling on her. Heat rushed through her veins as she realized he was applying the description to her instead of the land, a beautiful nothing. She pivoted to glare at him, all proud and defiant, her dark eyes flashing, her volatile beauty coming into play.

"On the other hand, maybe one of us isn't seeing it all," Travis qualified his previous statement.

His sun-browned features revealed nothing. Neither did his eyes. LaRaine was confused, unsure whether there was a double meaning to his comments or whether she had imagined it. Travis moved off toward the barn before she could decide.

LaRaine watched him go, with Sam following. She saw him say something to Sam, evidently about the bay horse, because Sam gathered the reins and led the horse inside the barn after Travis had slid the door open. An hour ago she would have smiled at that, aware of Sam's dread of horses. At that moment, the thought didn't even register.

When they came out of the barn they were discussing the proposed use of Travis's ranch as a location for the movie. Sam was doing most of the talking, explaining which sections of the ranch would be used and the approximate length of time it would take to film the location sequences. They discussed price and who would be responsible for what. The two men remained outside, standing on the porch, and LaRaine overheard it all.

When they came to terms, Sam shook Travis's hand. "It's a deal, then, McCrea. I'll have all the legal papers drawn up so you can review the agreement with our attorney. We should have our film crew out here next week if it's all satisfactory."

"Sounds good," Travis agreed noncommittally.

"I'll make a phone call and get the ball rolling." Sam excused himself, and entered the house.

His departure left a silence in its wake. LaRaine wandered with seeming aimlessness toward the porch where Travis stood, a shoulder leaning against one of the upright posts supporting the roof. His hat brim shadowed the upper part of his face, but she felt his gaze on her.

"You could have asked for more money," she told him. "You would have got it. Everyone on the production staff wants your ranch for the location shots now that they've seen it."

"I'm satisfied with the price and the terms. It's fair to both sides." His tone indicated that it was none of her business.

"I was just trying to be helpful." LaRaine shrugged, but she felt defensive and on edge.

"Thanks, but I'm old enough to make my own decisions," he said dryly.

"And how old is that?" she blurted, her gaze flickering to the distinguished streaks of white hair at his temples.

"Forty last month, and how old are you?" Travis countered without hesitation.

"Didn't anyone ever tell you it isn't polite for a gentleman to ask a lady her age?" LaRaine would have guessed that he was in his late thirties. She veiled her surprise at learning he was older than that. He didn't look it. There was so much vitality about him, so much untapped strength.

"I'm not a gentleman." But his answer implied that she wasn't a lady, either.

"I'm twenty-five, going on twenty-six." She wished she hadn't put it that way. It reminded her of a child who had to tack on the approaching year to appear older.

Sam chose that moment to return. "It's all in motion," he told Travis. "I'll be back in touch with you in the next day or two."

"Fine."

"I know you have work to do, so we won't keep you. Besides, we have to be heading back." Sam shook hands with him again. "We'll be seeing a lot of each other over the next month or two, so I won't say goodbye."

"It was a pleasure meeting you, Mr. McCrea," LaRaine offered with studied formality. Strangely enough, she was just as eager to leave the company of the rancher as she had been to seek it. It wasn't like her to fluctuate in her wishes.

"You, too, Miss Evans," was his bland response.

The four-wheel-drive Scout had crested the rise, leaving the ranchyard behind, before Sam directed a remark to LaRaine. "McCrea didn't turn out to be the pushover you thought he would, did he?" he said with smug satisfaction. "You're going to have a time trying to twist him around your finger."

"Who said I wanted to?" LaRaine would rather have died than admit differently to Sam.

It seemed to be an extraordinarily long and silent drive back to the motel in Delta that was serving as headquarters for the cast and crew. LaRaine was glad when Sam let her out at the entrance and went to complete his report on the meeting with Travis McCrea.

As she walked down the hallway to her room, a door near hers opened. Susan Winters, who had one of the charter parts in the film, stepped into the hall. She was a slim, attractive girl with honey-brown hair. An eyebrow lifted in recognition when she saw LaRaine.

"You're back," she announced.

The statement was so obvious that LaRaine simply nodded and slipped the key into the door lock. She wasn't in the mood for conversation. The only thought in her mind was to shower away the grit and dust from the rough ride.

"You should have left word where you were going." Susan followed LaRaine into her room, unbothered that she hadn't been invited. "Andy Pandy was upset when he couldn't find you," she said, using the cast's nickname for their director. "Luckily someone saw you leave with Sam or your name would have been mud."

"You mean it isn't?" LaRaine retorted cynically. The director's opinion of her had seemed to be pretty low since she arrived here. "Besides, it wasn't any of his business where I was. My free time is my own. I checked the shooting schedule and there was nothing posted for me today."

"That was before Chuck cut his leg and had to be

taken to the hospital for stitches. They had to abandon that scene and rearrange the schedule," Susan explained.

"What heroics was Chuck performing this time?" She derisively referred to the leading man and his penchant to prove what a macho figure he was.

"It was a totally graceless accident. He stepped on a rock, twisted his ankle and fell, cutting his leg on a piece of glass lying on the ground."

"I'll bet that isn't the story the press release will give," LaRaine commented, knowing it would be one to enhance the star's image. She sat on the edge of the bed and began tugging off her boots.

"What made you decide to go with Sam today? I thought you two were bitter enemies." Susan had an emery board in her hand and began filing at her nails.

"He's bitter. I'm not." She tossed the boots in a corner and began unbuttoning her blouse. "He was taking a ride out to the new location to see if it met with his approval and asked if I wanted to come along. I was more than willing to escape this dreary hole." Her gaze swept the room with disdain.

"What's the verdict on the new location? Did Sam tell you?" Susan moved to half stand against and half sit on the low chest of drawers.

"It looks like we'll be shooting out there next week." LaRaine took off her blouse and tossed it on the bed with careless disregard for its soiled condition and the cleanliness of the bed.

She was accustomed to someone picking up after her. When she was younger, it had been her mother. Later, there had been her cousin Laurie to rely on to clean up her messes. Lately, it had been maids or cleaning ladies. Her disregard for such things had long been a habit.

"This whole project has been chaos from the beginning," Susan declared. "No one is organized. Really, LaRaine, changing locations in the middle of filming, that proves it right there. It's no wonder that everyone keeps talking about the budget and delays."

"From what Sam said, I gather that the change of locations won't require any reshooting." LaRaine stepped out of the fawn leather culottes and left them lying on the floor.

Walking to the small closet, she took out her two robes, one a red caftan and the other a gold velour that zipped up the front. She hesitated in her choice before selecting the red. The gold she flung across the lone chair, not bothering to hang it back up. After slipping the caftan over her head, she walked into the adjoining bathroom and turned the water on in the tub.

"The new place is on somebody's ranch, isn't it?" Susan called, raising her voice to make herself heard above the running water.

"Yes." La Raine returned to the bedroom and began winding her shoulder-length black hair into a bun on top of her head, securing it with a comb and pins.

"I heard the guy that owns it's a bachelor. Did you meet him or just look around?" Susan eyed her curiously.

"We looked around and we met the owner." LaRaine answered the question and volunteered no more.

"And?" Susan prompted. "What was your impression?"

"You have to see the place to believe it." Her dark gaze swept the hotel room, comparing it to the ranch house and deciding it was a palace.

"Who cares about the place?" Susan dismissed that as totally unimportant. "I want to know about the man."

"You'll meet him yourself next week." LaRaine had no desire to discuss Travis McCrea.

"What does that mean—hands off, you saw him first?" the girl laughed with a trace of sarcastic challenge.

"It means," LaRaine walked to the bathroom door, "that I'm going to take a bath—in private."

Alone in the bathroom, LaRaine heard the hotel room door close, signaling that Susan had left. It wouldn't matter what she told Susan about Travis. The word would have spread that she was out to snare the rancher. Everyone expected her to go after any eligible bachelor that came along, especially the ones that were believed to be wealthy. It was true, wasn't it? So why did it bother her?

CHAPTER THREE

IT WAS ALMOST two full weeks before the movie company moved onto the McCrea ranch. Gossip had continued to be whispered throughout the cast and crew, linking LaRaine with the rancher, even though she had not seen him since that one time.

LaRaine ignored it. As intrigued as she had been with the man, Travis McCrea did not meet her standards. Just thinking about the house made her shudder. In her mind, she crossed him off her list. The problem was that there was no one left on her list who could be regarded as potential husband material.

Her future, beyond the conclusion of this film, looked bleak. Twice she had come close to catching the ideal man, only to lose him both times to someone else. She was afraid of failing a third time. Her confidence was shaken, although no one on the outside had guessed.

But then no one liked her, so they never bothered to find out how she truly felt about anything. That was the way she wanted it, she told herself. Who needed them anyway?

The film company was taking a noon break for lunch. The cast and crew intermingled, clustered in little groups around the film set. The director and his assistant were huddled with the screenwriter, going over more proposed script changes. A tangle of electric cords snaked along the ground, running from the lights and sound equipment to the generator truck.

LaRaine was alone, sitting on a flat rock apart from the others. Her back was turned to the luxurious motor homes parked to the side, provided for the leading actors in the film. Inside the large vans there were soft, cushioned chairs and couches, plus air-conditioned comfort. She didn't need to be reminded that she would never attain that status in her career.

The styrofoam cup in her hand contained iced tea, but the sun had warmed it to a tepid stage. She swirled it uninterestedly. The remains of a sandwich and its wrapper were on the ground near her feet, cast aside half-eaten.

It seemed like such a short time ago that she had shared an apartment with her cousin Laurie. At the time, LaRaine had been certain she could conquer the world. Now it seemed that the world was threatening to conquer her. Thick and long curling lashes touched to blink at the stinging moisture in her dark eyes. But her artfully made-up features retained their smooth, unemotional expression.

The drumming rhythm of a cantering horse opened her eyes. Approaching the film set were a horse and rider. LaRaine recognized the easy-riding man in the saddle immediately. Her gaze caught the slight checking of the reins by Travis McCrea that slowed the bay horse to a trot and finally a walk.

Unconsciously she got to her feet, discarding the cup on the ground. The tea spilled onto the thirsty soil. Her senses came to life, no longer dulled by the unhappiness of her thoughts. There was a faint quickening of her pulse as she watched him rein in at the edge of the set, not thirty feet from where she stood.

His gaze touched on her in silent recognition. LaRaine was drawn toward him, compelled by something she neither understood nor questioned. Others were aware of his arrival, but she didn't notice. As she walked forward, she admired his fluid dismount. Despite his height and muscled build, his movements held an animal grace, the suggestion of lightness almost catlike.

"Look what the wind blew in!" Her voice was riddled with cynical mockery and a trace of arrogance. "If it isn't our long, tall Texan!"

"Miss Evans." Leather-gloved fingers touched the dusty brim of his brown hat in a respectful greeting, yet she didn't like that knowing complacency in his look. "Why are you off by yourself?"

Instantly LaRaine was on the defensive. "I was having lunch. I prefer to eat alone," she stated, her spine stiffening rigidly.

"I thought you might have been waiting for me." The corners of his mouth deepened in amusement, but the half-smile seemed to taunt.

"But I didn't know you were coming." She kept her reply calm and smooth while she bristled inside.

"I thought your boyfriend might have mentioned it." Travis gave the impression of shrugging indifferently.

"My boyfriend?" LaRaine challenged.

"Sam Hardesty," Travis identified.

"He isn't my boyfriend." Her correction was cool and swift.

"That's right." He made a brief nod of remembrance. "You said you dumped him, didn't you?"

Which was almost literally what she had done once she was assured she had a small part in this film. She had been accused of such a thing before, but, coming from this man, it was a condemnation that hurt.

"No, I said that he asked me to marry him and I refused." She rephrased it to take out the sting of his sentence.

But the look in his dark brown eyes said that she had probably led Sam to believe that her answer would be affirmative. Maybe she had, but LaRaine would only admit that to herself. She rationalized her actions with the excuse that she needed the job. She had been desperate—and still was.

"I believe you did say that," Travis agreed, but his expression didn't change.

"Hello, Travis." Sam Hardesty hustled forward to shake his hand. "It's good to see you again."

"You left a message at the house that said you wanted to talk to me." Travis explained the reason why he was there.

"Yes, I did," Sam admitted. "We have a scene coming up next week that calls for cattle. I wondered if you would want to rent us about thirty head of your stock."

Neither man paid the slightest bit of attention to LaRaine standing beside them. She waited for Travis to snap up the offer, guessing that he was probably desperate for money considering the state his ranch buildings were in.

But he didn't. "What will you use the cattle for?" he questioned instead.

"We just need a small herd to be grazing in the background with a couple of cowboys working them maybe," Sam explained. "We won't be stampeding them or anything like that."

"In that case, I can gather thirty head for you," Travis agreed.

"Good, and the scruffier they look, the better," Sam added.

"All I have on the place is blooded stock," Travis told him. "If it's rough-looking range cattle you want, you'd better check with one of the other ranchers in the area."

"I see." Sam looked thoughtfully away, mulling over this information. "Maybe they'll work, anyway. I'll talk it over with the others," he said. "In the meantime, why don't you come over where the others are and I'll introduce you around?"

Travis hesitated as if he had more important things to do, then agreed, "All right."

"Do you want a cup of coffee, a sandwich or anything?" Sam offered. "The mobile canteen is here."

"Nothing, thank you," he refused.

LaRaine walked along with them. She noticed the way heads turned as the lunching cast and crew noticed Travis walking through their midst leading his big bay horse. It wasn't just because he was a stranger. It had something to do with that air of quiet authority about him, a presence that made itself felt. She couldn't help thinking that it was a pity he wasn't rich.

"How is the calf?" She sought his attention because it was something she sensed the other female members would like to have. "Did it live?" She remembered how pathetically weak it had been.

His bland gaze swung to her, running over the made-up perfection of her face. "Yes, it lived," he answered, and looked straight ahead. "It's blind in one eye, but it's getting around all right."

"If it's blind, you won't turn it loose, will you?" The thought of the helpless calf wandering about the waste-land that surrounded them made LaRaine frown.

Again his gaze inspected her face, amused yet curious at her response. "The calf lost the sight in only one eye. He'll make out all right," he assured her.

"That's heartless!" LaRaine declared in a tautly controlled voice.

Sam had been listening in on the conversation. "Coming from you, LaRaine, that's rich," he laughed.

"Nóbody asked your opinion, Sam." She shot him an angry look, the insult stinging because it had been made in front of Travis. She didn't understand why that mattered. Hadn't she decided she wasn't interested in him?

Sam directed their path to where a couple of members of his staff were seated, and LaRaine stood to one side as he introduced Travis. She noticed how at ease Travis seemed in surroundings that must be strange to him. As far as she could tell, he wasn't in awe of those around him. She remembered when he'd met her, how indifferent he'd been to her supposedly glamorous profession. In some ways, it was a consolation to discover that he treated the others the same way he had treated her.

The bay horse stomped at a fly buzzing around its hocks, its head bobbing down to its knee to brush it off with its nose. The sleek, mahogany hide shivered to chase away the flying pests. LaRaine admired again its conformation and the rippling muscles in its chest and hindquarters.

"What's the matter, feller?" she murmured, and stroked her hand along its neck and withers. "Are the flies bothering you, mmm?"

Its head turned to rub its forelock against her shoulder. Smiling at the action, she took a step away to scratch the spot on its forehead. The horse inhaled her scent and blew softly through its nose.

"You like that, do you?" LaRaine crooned. "You're a big, beautiful brute. Do you know that?"

The horse bobbed its head, but it was to chase away another fly and not a response to her low question. LaRaine chose to pretend that it was, playing a childish game in her mind.

"Aren't you worried that he might hurt you, Miss Evans?" The question from Travis made her suddenly aware that he was watching her. "He outweighs you by several hundred pounds."

"No, I'm not worried." It was easier for LaRaine to keep looking at the horse than to glance at Travis. "I like horses. What's his name?"

"Dallas."

"Is that where you're from? Dallas, Texas?" This time she did look at him, her glance curious, but when she met his gaze, a crazy sensation raced through her nerve ends, a tingling awareness of his rugged virility.

"No, I bought him, from a Mormon rancher. He named him, I didn't," Travis answered.

"He's a beautiful animal. I'd like to ride him sometime." LaRaine wasn't angling for an invitation when she said it, but she realized afterward that it probably sounded as if she was.

"Sorry, he's a working horse, not a pleasure mount." Travis turned her down gently but nonetheless firmly.

"Which means you think he's more horse than I can handle," she concluded. "I'm not a novice. All the same, I understand your unwillingness to let just anybody ride him. If he were mine, I wouldn't, either."

"I'm glad you understand my reasons," he said.

Sam interrupted their conversation to include Travis in a discussion he was having with one of the staff. LaRaine continued to stroke the bay horse absently while covertly watching Travis. She became fascinated with the powerful line of his profile, strong and bold. His skin was stretched tautly over his bones like a tanned hide, and was almost the same color.

The smoothness of his sun-hardened features was marred only by crinkling lines around his eyes and the grooves running from nose to mouth. In an actor, LaRaine would have suspected the silver streaks in Travis's hair just above his ears had been professionally dyed. But there seemed nothing artificial or fake about this man who was all man.

As she studied him, she noticed his gaze narrow. He seemed to be looking beyond the small circle of men, and she glanced around to see what had attracted his attention. Susan Winters had just walked by, but other than that, everything looked the same as it had only minutes ago.

LaRaine looked back at Travis and realized his gaze was following Susan. His expression changed from piercing scrutiny to frowning disbelief and then wary recognition, one right after the other. LaRaine glanced at Susan. Did Travis know her? How?

In the next second Travis was walking past her, his long strides taking him after Susan. His abrupt departure from Sam and his group left them in stunned silence. Like LaRaine, they stared after him, puzzled and surprised.

"Natalie?" Travis called out the name in a questioning voice. As he drew closer to Susan, he repeated it with more certainty. "Natalie!"

LaRaine realized he was referring to Susan by that name, but Susan continued to walk on, unaware that anyone was trying to get her attention. She yelped in surprise when Travis caught up with her and grabbed her arm to turn her around to face him.

"Natalie, I—"

"What are you doing?" Susan struggled against the grip he had on her shoulders and tipped her head to look up at him, her honey-brown hair swinging away from her face.

Travis didn't complete the sentence he had started. LaRaine could almost see the poised stillness come over him. It lasted only as long as it took him to examine Susan's face. Abruptly he released her and took a step away. His features hardened into granite to control his expression so it wouldn't reveal what he was thinking or feeling. "Sorry," he apologized curtly. "I thought you were someone else."

"You're sorry? You scared me to death!" Susan laughed, a trifle breathlessly, but she was talking to air.

Travis had already pivoted away and was striding back to where LaRaine stood beside his horse. Silence dominated Sam and his group. His rock-hard expression kept anyone from joking about his mistake. It also kept them from saying anything.

The reins had been left to drag on the ground. When Travis reached the group, he scooped the dangling reins up in his gloved hand. LaRaine's fingers curved inside the cheek strap of the bridle, instinctively holding the bay horse.

Travis's gaze swung to the group, specifically to Sam. "I have to get back to work. Let me know if you decide you want to use my cattle."

"Sure thing, Travis." Sam was plainly intimidated.

Travis didn't wait for the response as he looped the reins over the bay's head and slipped a toe into the stirrup to swing into the saddle. LaRaine still had a hold of the bridle. She checked his attempt to rein the horse away from the group. She wasn't intimidated. Her curiosity was too thoroughly aroused to let it go unsatisfied. His hooded gaze slid to her.

"Who did you think Susan was?" she demanded.

"Susan?" There was initial blankness before he realized she was referring to the girl he had thought was someone named Natalie. His mouth thinned. "Isn't it obvious?" His question was almost a jeer. "I thought she was someone else," he snapped.

This time he touched a spur to the bay's ribs. The

horse jumped out of LaRaine's hold, spinning around on its hindquarters. It took one bounding leap forward before its rider checked its speed to a running walk.

LaRaine watched him go, his back ramrod straight. As he rode off the set, a murmur of voices began to swell. Everyone who had witnessed the scene was talking about it. Travis's answer hadn't satisfied LaRaine, it only whetted her already aroused curiosity. She resolved to find out what it was all about some day, and to find out who this Natalie person was.

When Susan came up to her, LaRaine was still watching the horse and rider growing steadily smaller. She barely glanced at Susan. Her interest was completely captured by the departing figure.

"Who was he?" Susan questioned. "Don't tell me he's the man who owns this ranch?"

"Yes, he is," LaRaine admitted. As he disappeared from sight, her preoccupied gaze swung to Susan.

"No wonder you kept your opinion about him such a deep, dark secret," Susan commented. "What's his name?"

There was no reason to withhold the information. Susan could find it out from someone else easily enough. It took a couple of seconds for LaRaine to get his name out.

"Travis McCrea."

"Travis." Susan repeated the name as if testing the sound of it. "I wonder who he thought I was."

"Somebody else, obviously." LaRaine used his answer, her voice as dry and biting as his had been.

"Yes, but I wonder who?" Susan repeated the question, her expression thoughtful.

"Maybe you looked like his sister." She was suddenly impatient with the questions, the very same questions that were running through her own mind.

"No, not his sister," Susan replied with certainty. "The way he was looking at me before he discovered I wasn't this Natalie would have melted any woman's bones. Whoever Natalie is, she isn't his sister."

"So? Maybe she's an old girl friend." LaRaine shrugged as if this Natalie's relationship to Travis was of no interest to her, when in actuality she was consumed by it.

"I'll tell you one thing—I wish I had been Natalie," Susan declared.

"You aren't, so what's the sense in going on about it?" LaRaine retorted.

"Because that Travis McCrea is one hunk of a man. I thought you had the inside track on him." The brown-haired girl measured LaRaine with a look. "But I don't think you do. I think I have a better chance with him than you do."

"Why? Just because you look like someone he might have once been in love with?" LaRaine challenged with a brash air of unconcern. Inwardly, she was afraid that Susan was right.

"Sure. Why not?" Susan reasoned. "It's certain I have his attention. I think I'll invite him to the party we're having next weekend. I'll bet he accepts."

"You're too late. I've already invited him," LaRaine lied.

"You have?" Susan frowned, her disappointment showing. "Is he coming?"

"What do you think?" she retorted, making it

deliberately sound positive before she turned to walk away.

Susan caught her arm. "Is he really coming with you?" she demanded.

"If you don't believe me, ask him yourself the next time you see him." LaRaine returned the girl's skeptical look with one of cool reproof.

"You always have to go after every new man that comes along, don't you, LaRaine?" Susan accused.

"That's certainly the pot calling the kettle black," LaRaine mocked. "You've just admitted that you're going to chase him."

"There's a big difference between you and me. I want to go out with Travis McCrea because I like him, but you want to see what you can get out of him. Do you think maybe he has some influence somewhere and may be able to get you a part in some movie? It's certain you won't be able to trick Sam again."

"Has Sam been crying on your shoulder?" LaRaine pretended that the remark hadn't hurt.

"He's talked to me about you, yes," Susan admitted.

"Then I hope he told you that I never asked him to get me this job," she retorted.

"Maybe not, but you gave him the impression that you wanted it so the two of you wouldn't be separated."

"That might have been in his mind, but it wasn't in mine," LaRaine denied the accusation.

"I'm sure it wasn't." Sarcasm inched into Susan's voice. "What's in your mind regarding Travis McCrea?"

"Maybe I just want to keep in practice until something better comes along," LaRaine offered as her possible reason.

Anger reddened the other girl's face. "If he's stupid enough to be taken in by you, I don't want him." Susan turned on her heel and stalked away.

LaRaine's gaze followed her. People were so easily maneuvered sometimes, she thought. With just a few well-chosen words, she had eliminated her competition. Susan had gone from wanting to invite Travis to a party to throwing him in LaRaine's lap.

Why had she claimed that Travis was going to the party with her? LaRaine sighed. Had it been because she saw someone else wanted him? Sometimes she didn't understand her motives, if she had any. Even now she didn't understand why she was doing all this soul-searching over her actions.

Either way, she had committed herself to persuading Travis McCrea to go to the party with her next week. Maybe it wasn't such a bad idea. He might not be husband material, but neither was anyone else around here. However, he would certainly be a diversion. LaRaine decided that she had been taking her life a little too seriously. Maybe it was time she had some fun.

Travis McCrea could be quite a challenge. Again, she wondered who Natalie was. From what Susan had said, it must have been someone he cared about a great deal. Obviously he still did, if his reaction when he had mistaken Susan for her was anything to go by.

If he were still in love with her, then he wouldn't want to become serious. LaRaine shied away from possessive men who didn't have anything to offer in the long run. Sam Hardesty had become very tiresome with his broken heart permanently on display.

Maybe she could establish some kind of casual relationship with Travis McCrea. Until this moment she hadn't considered going to the party next week. Her mother had schooled it into her head that she should never go to any party without a date. But if she could persuade Travis to go with her, LaRaine suspected she would be the envy of every girl there, if today's reaction to him were repeated.

Just for a minute, LaRaine let her spirits droop. What difference did it make if they envied her? None of them liked her. If she fell on her face, they would all cheer and congratulate the one who knocked her down.

Why was she suddenly wishing it weren't that way? LaRaine breathed in deeply and released a long sigh.

CHAPTER FOUR

TWO NIGHTS in a row, LaRaine had attempted to contact Travis by telephone to invite him to the party the following week. The phone rang and rang, but no one answered. LaRaine decided that if she couldn't reach him by telephone she would have to find another way.

Her name wasn't on the day's shooting schedule. Skirting the film set, she walked to the horse vans where the actors' horses were kept in readiness. The remuda boss was sitting on a bale of hay in the shade of one of the vans.

"Hi, Don." She was wearing the same split riding skirt and blouse that she had worn the first time she had met Travis. "Is anybody using the palomino today?"

He tipped his hat back and looked up at her. "Nope."

"Good. I thought I'd take him out for a ride. The palomino needs the exercise almost as much as I do," LaRaine said.

"You know I'm not supposed to let anyone take these horses out," Don reminded her, his cheek bulging with a wad of tobacco.

"I know the whole insurance routine," she nodded. "I promise I won't sue the company if I get hurt. If a horse throws me, it's probably my fault anyway. So what do you say, Don? Will you let me ride the palomino?" A flat-crowned hat, protection against the sun while she was riding, dangled down her back.

"If it were anyone else but you asking, I'd turn them down," he said, and turned his head to spit out a stream of tobacco juice. The remuda boss was a former stunt man; his career ended when an accident crippled his leg.

"Don't tell me that you trust me, Don?" LaRaine laughed. "That makes you a minority of one around here."

He smiled briefly at that and pushed himself to his feet.

"I don't know as how I'd trust you with my money, but I do trust you with my horses."

"I don't understand your logic. But as long as you're going to let me ride the palomino, I don't care whether or not it makes any sense," she declared.

"You wait here and I'll bring him," Don ordered, and limped away.

Fifteen minutes later, LaRaine was astride the palomino and riding off in the direction of the ranchyard two miles away. The horse was spirited and eager to cover ground, but responsive to its rider's commands.

Picking up the rutted trail, LaRaine followed it to the ranchyard, cantering the horse where the terrain was relatively smooth and slowing it down to a walk or trot where it was rougher. She doubted that she would be lucky enough to find Travis at the house.

The place looked deserted when she rode in. She walked the palomino to the house, dismounted and tied the reins around a porch post. She knocked at the door, but there wasn't any answer.

Leaving the palomino tied, she walked to the barn. The wide double doors stood open, sunlight invading part of the darkened interior. As she entered, her boots made a rustling sound on the straw-covered floor. From one of the stalls, a calf bawled. LaRaine followed the sound to a stall closed in with a gate.

It took a minute for her eyes to adjust to the dimness. Then she saw the red calf curled up in the straw. Its white face turned to her, scarred with purple medication spotting its white hair. She glimpsed its gnarled eye, but the calf still looked considerably better than it had the last time she had seen it. It made a low, bleating sound at the sight of her.

"At least he hasn't turned you loose yet, little feller." Her mouth quirked in the semblance of a smile. "Where did he go? Do you know?"

The calf continued to stare at her. Sighing, LaRaine turned away from the barn and walked back into the sunlight of the outside. She slipped her hat off, letting it hang down her back, held by the rawhide thong around her throat. She wondered where Travis might be.

Trying to find him in this desolate country without knowing where to look would be ridiculous. It would be too easy to get lost. It all looked alike to LaRaine—sage and grass-covered land bounded by juniper-studded mountains with a multitude of canyons and sweeping valleys. LaRaine paused, shading her eyes with her hand. There didn't seem to be a sign of life anywhere. She walked to where the palomino stood and untied the reins. Mounting, she turned it away from the house and hesitated. Maybe if she made a sweeping arc around the ranchyard, while staying within sight of it, she might catch a glimpse of Travis. It was worth a try, she decided.

Urging the palomino into a canter, she started out, making a wide circle away from the buildings. Her gaze skimmed the landscape, unimpressed by the wild terrain. A long-eared jackrabbit raced alongside her for a while and then made a lightning-quick right angle turn to disappear into the sage. LaRaine ignored it, as she ignored the chukar that took flight at the palomino's approach.

She had almost decided that her attempt to find Travis would be fruitless when she caught a movement in her side vision and reined the palomino to a stop. It pranced in protest while she tried to locate what had momentarily caught her attention.

Far back in an arroyo she saw the object, or objects as it turned out to be. The distinctive red color and shape of Hereford cattle took form in the sage and brush-covered gully. They were ambling to the mouth of the arroyo. LaRaine was about to ride on when she saw the horse and rider driving the dozen or so head of cattle. It was Travis. She felt she would recognize him anywhere.

A smile curved her mouth as she turned the palomino and started it down the incline that would take her to the valley floor and eventually to the mouth of the arroyo. Once down the slope, she had to wind her way through the thick stands of brush, relying on her sense of direction to guide her to her destination. It proved fairly reliable. Travis was just riding out of the mouth when she intersected his path and reined her horse alongside his. Surprise flickered briefly in his eyes.

"Hello." There was triumph in her greeting. The taste of successfully finding him was sweet.

"Are you lost?" Amusement glittered in the sideways look he gave her.

"If I were, I'm not anymore. You've found me." LaRaine arched him a smiling look.

"What are you doing out here?" he questioned.

"I was looking for you," she replied truthfully.

"Oh?" The simple word asked for an explanation.

A mottled gray dog with a black face barked at a straying cow and chased it back with the others. The palomino danced nervously at the swift gray shadow of the cattle dog.

"I wanted to prove to you that I could ride," she answered after easily bringing her mount under control and slowing it to a sedate walk beside his horse. This time he was riding a buckskin. It was almost the same size as the bay, but it lacked the finer points of conformation that the bay possessed.

"I believed you," said Travis.

"Did you? You looked skeptical when I told you," she accused, but without malice. "Who is your friend?" She nodded to the dog.

"Blue is my working partner, a blue heeler." When Travis spoke his name, the dog looked around, its ears pricking. Deciding there wasn't going to be any command, the dog returned to its business of keeping the cattle grouped and moving forward.

"Do you run this ranch by yourself?" she questioned, a finely arched brow lifting into a frown.

"No, I have a hired hand who works for me. He's the younger son of one of my neighbors. A hard-working boy."

"Boy?" LaRaine questioned the term.

"He's nineteen. From my view, that's young," Travis explained dryly.

"I'd forgotten how old you are," she mocked. "Is that your bones I hear creaking, or the saddle?"

"This time it's the saddle." A cow threatened to elude the dog and take off into the sage. Travis reined his horse to pursue it, but the dog turned it back with the others.

"The buckskin isn't as good a horse as the bay," LaRaine observed, unconsciously attempting to show off her knowledge of horses.

"Not in looks maybe," Travis conceded. "But he's strong and dependable, and tough as nails. Looks alone don't count for much out here." His gaze was on her when he said the last. LaRaine had the feeling the comment was directed at her.

"Did you buy him here?" Uncertain how to take the remark, she kept the conversation centered on the horse.

"In Utah, yes," he nodded.

"From the same man who sold you the bay?"

"No, I've only had the buckskin a year. I bought the bay two years ago when I moved here," Travis answered.

"Two years ago?" She eyed him curiously. "You mean you've only owned this ranch for two years?"

"That's right." Travis never let his attention become diverted for long from the cattle.

"Did you have a ranch in Texas?" LaRaine had difficulty visualizing Travis working for someone else.

"No. I managed ranches. I finally decided it was time I put in all those long hours on a place of my own. So I took my savings, came here, and bought this ranch, such as it is. But it's mine." There was a quiet pride in the statement.

"Why did you come here? Why didn't you stay in Texas?" LaRaine thought she knew the answer, but she waited to hear what he had to say.

"I felt there was more opportunity here." His look dared her to challenge his answer.

For the time being, LaRaine didn't. "Where did you work in Texas?" she asked instead.

"Do you want my life history, is that it?" His slanted smile seemed to taunt, but he answered, "I was born in the Panhandle of Texas, worked as a hand on one of the ranches there after I graduated from high school. Then I moved to a ranch in the hill country outside of San Antonio. After a few years I took over the management of that ranch." He seemed to hesitate. "A friend of mine was hurt in a plane crash, so I ran his place in west Texas until he recovered. Then I came here."

"Your friend who was hurt, was his wife's name Natalie?" LaRaine questioned, certain that faint pause, and the tightness of his voice, had given it away.

He glanced at her and smiled slowly. "Cord's wife is named Stacy."

"Who is Natalie?" she persisted in treading on what she guessed was forbidden ground.

"She's a woman I know," was all he admitted.

"And you loved her?" LaRaine questioned.

His look was hard and impatient. "I love her," but his voice was calm.

LaRaine noticed that he didn't use the past tense. "What happened?"

"That, Miss Evans, is none of your business," he said flatly.

And she knew it was foolish to try to make him relent from his stand. She let both hands rest on the saddle horn, the reins loose around the horse's neck.

"I think I asked you before to call me LaRaine, didn't I?" she asked with mock innocence.

"I believe you did." Travis nodded and looked straight ahead at the red backs of the cattle.

"And?" LaRaine let her gaze rest on the golden head of her horse as it bobbed back and forth in rhythm with its walking stride.

"I'll try to remember the next time—LaRaine." He stressed her name with mocking emphasis.

"You wouldn't happen to have some water in your canteen, would you?" she asked. "I'm thirsty and I forgot to bring any."

"You should never go riding in this country without it," Travis stated, and reined his horse to a stop. "You never know when it might save your life."

LaRaine stopped her horse. "I'll remember that the next time."

With a hand signal, Travis gave a command to the dog, and LaRaine watched with fascination as it circled the cattle and forced them to stop without spooking a single one of them. There was plenty of yellow grass growing amidst the clumps of sage. The Herefords were content to graze.

When she glanced at Travis, she discovered he had dismounted and was removing his canteen from the saddlebags. LaRaine started to dismount, then changed her mind when she saw Travis walking around his horse to her left side. She realized he was going to do the gentlemanly thing and help her down.

It was an opportunity that she didn't intend to pass up. She swung her right leg over the saddle horn as his large hands reached up to span her waist. Kicking her left boot free of the stirrup, she placed her hands on his broad shoulders for balance. He lifted her as easily as he had carried the calf.

When her feet touched the ground, LaRaine swayed toward him. Her hands, instead of gliding down his chest, curved around his neck. As she tipped her head back and to the side, a sultry, enticing look darkened her eyes. The glistening sheen of her lips was offered to him. Every move was deliberate and calculated to invite an embrace.

Travis's hands rested loosely on her waist, neither holding nor rejecting. He looked down at her upturned face. His expression revealed an aloof kind of dry amusement as he made no move to accept her invitation.

LaRaine had expected this initial, passive resistance. She slid her fingers into the thickly curled black strands of hair at the back of his neck to force his head down. Travis submitted to the pressure, but it was a slow descent.

The touch of his hard lips on hers was warm and undemanding. Her pulse quickened in excitement. Travis was proving to be as susceptible to her practiced charm as others had been. His mouth moved experimentally over hers, yet there was nothing tentative about the kiss.

Slowly, LaRaine let herself begin to relax against him. It was like leaning against a stone statue warmed by the sun. Her intent was to deepen the kiss and introduce a seductive passion to the embrace. But before her lips could make their demand on him, his leather-gloved hand moved to capture her chin and hold it still.

The initiative had been hers, but now Travis was taking over. He held control over which direction the kiss would take, and he chose to avoid passion. His mouth continued its exploration of hers, mobilely investigating its pliant softness and taunting its parted invitation. The firm pressure was subtly teasing, frustrating LaRaine with its promise of satisfaction that was not fulfilled.

She was not free to respond but only to feel. A multitude of sensations began crowding into her mind. The hot sun had dampened his skin with perspiration, intensifying the odors that clung to his shirt. The smell of leather and horseflesh mingled with a lingering brutish scent of shaving lotion, then intermixed with the individual male smell of him to form a potent combination.

Her arms around his neck made LaRaine aware of the even rise and fall of his solid chest. The large hand resting at her side encompassed both the curve of her waist and her hip bone, its grip relaxed and unrestrictive. The hand cupping her chin was firm, implying a

strength that could snap her slender neck as easily
as a toothpick. Most of all her sensitive nerve ends
were aware of the male length of him from the
sinewy hard columns of his long legs to the muscled
brawn of his chest and shoulders—masculinity in
its perfect state, virilely male and powerfully constructed.

There was a fluttering weakness in her stomach. For
the first time in her life, LaRaine wanted to respond
naturally to a man's kiss. It was no longer a part of
some grand design to maneuver a man into giving her
what she wanted. The irregular beat of her heart
drummed the discovery into her mind.

This unexpected longing quivered through her. It
was a slight movement, barely discernible, yet Travis
must have felt it. For a fraction of a second his mouth
was motionless in its possession of hers. Then he was
slowly lifting his head and relaxing his hold of her chin.
Her long, curling lashes drifted open. Confused disappointment was in her dark eyes for Travis to see, but
his shuttered look revealed nothing.

Unwinding her arms from around his neck, he
brought them down and held them to make a space between them. Shaken by the sensuous experience,
LaRaine lowered her gaze to her hands; her wrists were
lost in the loose hold of his gloved hands.

"Are you bored, LaRaine?" His voice taunted.
"Are you seeking a diversion, an affair with a local
cowboy to pass the time?"

She drew her wrists free of his hold and turned, taking a step away. That had been her plan. Only now,
everything seemed to be turned upside down, but the

veiled attack was just what LaRaine needed to regain control of her confused senses.

"I don't know," her initial response was truthful. "Maybe I am." Over her shoulder she cast him a glance sideways, a look filled with coy arrogance. "If I were what would you say?"

Amusement twitched the corners of his mouth, as if he found something about her challenge humorous. "That there are still men around who prefer to do the chasing."

"Men are sometimes so slow," LaRaine shrugged. "A girl can get tired of waiting for him to catch up with her."

Travis didn't respond to that. Slipping the canteen strap off his arm, he unscrewed the lid. "Do you still want that drink?" His tone doubted that she had been thirsty in the first place.

"I do, yes." She reached out to take the canteen from his hand.

Tipping her head back, she lifted the canteen to her lips and let the warm water trickle down her throat. While she was drinking, Travis removed his dusty brown hat and hooked it over the horn of her saddle. With his fingers he combed the springing thickness of his black hair and smoothed it into the silver wings at the side.

Finished with the canteen, LaRaine handed it back to him. "This is the first time I've seen you without a hat," she observed. Except for the white at his temples, there wasn't a trace of gray anywhere else in his dark hair. "I was beginning to wonder whether or not you were bald."

His mouth twisted into a half-smile, the canteen poised midway. "Do you always say what's on your mind?"

"I've always understood that men like frankness in a woman." She studied the hand holding the canteen. It was covered with a work-worn leather glove, but it didn't disguise its size. She wondered what it would be like to be caressed by his hands, whether they could arouse her in that same strange, new way that his kiss had.

"Who told you that?" Travis had taken his drink and was recapping the canteen.

LaRaine shrugged. "It's something I learned through personal experience and observation. I don't know if it's really true. But I do know that it attracts attention and I'm never ignored."

"As long as you don't forget that a little goes a long way." He put his hat back on, pulling the brim down low in front. Walking to the palomino's head, he took hold of the bridle and glanced at LaRaine. "Are you ready to move on?"

"I guess so," she agreed, and walked over to mount her horse.

His hand gripped her elbow to help her aboard. Then Travis was passing her the reins and walking over to mount his buckskin. He whistled to the dog lying alertly on the ground near the grazing cattle. Within seconds the rider and dog had the cattle moving.

"Where are you taking them?" LaRaine questioned.

"To the corral by the barn. Sam decided it would be more feasible to use my livestock than have the expense of another rancher bringing his in," he explained.

"He needs more than these, doesn't he?" Making a rough count, LaRaine doubted if there were two more than a dozen.

"Blue and I will drive these in and get another bunch." His gaze swung from the small herd to her. "Why aren't you working? Aren't they filming today?"

"Yes, but I'm not in any of the scenes we're shooting. My part isn't very large." Which was putting it mildly.

"Are you waiting to be discovered?" he inquired in a jesting tone.

"I've already been discovered." LaRaine found herself answering his question with unusual honesty. "The trouble is that the same time they discovered me, they found out I wasn't another Helen Hayes. I can't act my way out of a paper bag."

"How did you get this part?"

"Through Sam," she admitted. "He used his influence to get it for me."

"Because he loved you," Travis stated dryly.

She faced him, her chin held high in defiant challenge, pride stamped in her features. "Yes, because he loved me. It sounds like a dirty trick, doesn't it? But I needed a job—I needed it desperately. I never lied to Sam, though. I never told him I loved him or promised him anything." She couldn't tell what he was thinking. His expression was masked. She looked straight ahead. "I always dreamed of being a famous movie star. When I was offered my first role, I grabbed at it. Because of that, my fiance broke our engagement and ultimately married my cousin. Now I realize I'll never be a famous actress. I'm just hanging on."

"What will you do when this movie is over?"

"Find me a rich man and marry him." After she had said it, LaRaine laughed. Her dark eyes danced with mischief when she glanced at Travis. "If you'd been rich, I would have married you."

"Why are you telling me this? Is this part of your frankness?" There was amusement in the look he returned to her.

"No." She considered her answer before she gave it. "There are some men that you can't hide things from. They find out anyway. I think you're one of those men. If I didn't tell you, you'd guess. You might as well know where I stand."

"I see," he murmured noncommittally.

"Do you? Good, because there's a party next week that some of the cast and crew are having. I'd like you to come with me," she invited.

"No." His refusal was short and to the point.

"Oh." She let out the breath in a sigh. "I have a problem, then."

"What's that?" Travis sliced her an impersonal look.

"I've already told everybody that you're taking me," she admitted without a hint of regret.

Travis chuckled in disbelief. "What is this? Are you trying to trap me into taking you so you won't be caught lying?"

"It's more a case of putting my foot in my mouth. It's a recurring disease I have. Will you help me out?" LaRaine knew it was an audacious tactic, but she sensed that boldness was the only thing Travis would appreciate.

The ranch buildings were in sight. Travis reined in his horse and whistled a signal to the dog. When the cattle had stopped moving, he looked across his shoulder at LaRaine. She waited as his inscrutable gaze skimmed her face.

"It seems I've always been easy prey for women who are in trouble and need help," he said at last.

Somehow, LaRaine had the feeling his thoughts weren't on her. He was thinking about that girl named Natalie. She thought she caught a glimmer of pain in his faraway look.

"Then you'll take me to the party?" she breathed out the question.

"Yes, but don't try to use me, LaRaine. You won't get away with it," he warned.

"Good." LaRaine bit at her lower lip to contain her bursting triumph. "I'd better be getting back. Technically, I'm not supposed to be riding this horse." She told him which day it was and what time he could pick her up and where.

With a wave of her hand she started toward the dirt road beyond the ranch buildings. Travis left the herd with the dog and rode to open the corral gate. Before she was out of sight, LaRaine saw the horse and rider and dog driving the cattle into the enclosure.

CHAPTER FIVE

THE MEETING WITH TRAVIS had surpassed her wildest expectations. Outside of those unsettling moments of his kiss, she had controlled everything. Travis had not proved as formidable as she had thought he might, but he hadn't attempted to match wits with her, either.

It wouldn't be wise to underestimate him. LaRaine ran her fingers over her lips, remembering how his mouth had felt when it had explored them. How seductively he had mastered her and made her respond differently physically than she had with any other man. In many ways, Travis was still an unknown element. She had to feel her way.

The palomino quickened its pace as it crested the hill and saw the horse van ahead and his fellow equine companions. LaRaine didn't try to hold him back, letting him canter in. She was in such a good mood that when she saw Sam walking forward to meet her, she waved and smiled. He didn't return it. In fact, when she stopped her horse near him, Sam was glowering.

"I might have known you were out riding," he accused.

"What's the matter, Sam? Were you worried about me?" she joked, and swung lightly out of the saddle.

"No, I wasn't worried about you," Sam denied. "I wouldn't waste my time that way."

LaRaine laughed, a throaty, practiced sound. "You sound angry about something, Sam. What is it?" She stroked the palomino's neck, patting its sleek coat, only faintly warm from the ride.

"I'll tell you what it is," he began, only to be interrupted by a strident male voice issuing a demand.

"Where have you been, Miss Evans?"

Turning, LaRaine saw the director puffing toward her. His roly-poly face was livid with rage. She was certain he was going to burst a blood vessel in his neck any minute.

"I went for a ride, Mr. Behr." Her tone was respectful, not mocking him the way she did Sam. The cast and crew called the director Andy Pandy behind his back, but never to his face.

"Who gave you permission to take that horse?" he demanded.

"No one. I wanted to go riding, so I checked to see which horse wasn't being used today and took him." LaRaine didn't say it had been the remuda boss who had given her that information.

"It so happens we rewrote the scene and needed that horse. Only you'd taken it!" the director accused angrily. "Without asking anybody! Without telling anybody where you were going—or when you'd be back!"

Obviously Don, the remuda boss, hadn't told him that he'd saddled the palomino for her. If she expected him to do any more favors for her, LaRaine knew that she didn't dare tell the director otherwise.

"No, I'm sorry. I didn't," she lied, and remained calm and cool in the face of his anger.

"You're sorry!" he exploded. "You're not only a lousy actress, you're a disruptive influence as well. You pull another stunt like this and you'll find out what sorry means!" He flashed a look at Sam and snapped an order, "Bring that horse, Hardesty."

Turning on his heel, he puffed his way back toward the area where the cameras were set up. Sam watched him go, his mouth open in empty protest. LaRaine smiled, knowing how much Sam abhorred the four-footed beasts.

"Here, Sam." She offered him the reins to lead the palomino.

He closed his mouth and turned around, eyeing her coldly. "He means it, LaRaine. You cross him one more time and you'll regret it."

"If that happens, don't worry, Sam. I'll make sure he doesn't blame you for getting me this part," LaRaine taunted with false indifference.

While he seethed impotently, she pressed the reins into his hand and walked away. She knew she was walking a fine line with the director. Twice now she had been indirectly responsible for upsetting his schedule, once when she had gone with Sam to the McCrea ranch and now this time.

Andrew Behr was the kind of man who tolerated no excuses, however legitimate or justified they were. LaRaine had to be extra careful from now on. She couldn't risk the humiliation of being thrown off the set.

Soberly, LaRaine walked away. She wasn't in the

mood to hang around the film set. She didn't want to risk accidently incurring the director's wrath again by being underfoot in the wrong place. She saw Susan off to one side in costume and makeup. Fixing an uncaring expression on her face, she walked over to the girl.

"Hi, Susan. May I borrow your car? I thought I'd go back to the motel. You can catch a ride with somebody when you're through, can't you?" she reasoned. LaRaine's own car had been sold several months ago because she had needed the money more than the transportation.

"What's the matter? Are you afraid Andy Pandy might bite instead of snarl if you stay around here?" Susan guessed accurately.

"Andy is a pussycat if you know how to handle him," LaRaine lied. "It's too boring around here, that's all."

"My keys are in my bag over in Makeup. Tell Anna I said it was okay for you to take them," Susan gave in.

After obtaining the keys, LaRaine drove the battered Volkswagen back to the hotel. It was hardly luxury transport, but under the circumstances, LaRaine was grateful for that.

There was mail waiting for her when she stopped at the desk. She leafed through the envelopes as she walked to her room. They contained bills mostly and her bank statement. In her room, she opened the latter first. There was a slip inside, informing LaRaine that her account was overdrawn.

Sighing, she stared at the notice, then picked up the telephone on the stand beside the bed. LaRaine dialed the operator and placed a long-distance collect call to her agent. She heard the ring of impatience in his voice when he accepted the charges.

"Hi, Peter. It's LaRaine," she identified herself unnecessarily. She forced herself to sound cheerful. Not more than two hours ago after leaving Travis, she had been flushed with victory, but that sensation was easily punctured by the reality of finances. "How's the weather?"

"Smoggy. I hope you didn't phone me to discuss the weather, LaRaine," he sighed.

"Business, business, business—that's all you think about, Peter," LaRaine laughed, but it echoed hollowly in her ears.

"Please get to the point. I'm busy," he stated.

"Naturally I didn't call to talk about the weather," she said. He wasn't making this easy. "I have a slight problem."

"Let me guess," her agent insisted dryly. "You need money, don't you?"

She swallowed nervously, but spoke calmly. "Not very much," she admitted.

"How much is not very much?" he demanded.

"My bank account is overdrawn. If you could advance me a couple of thousand dollars—"

"Two thousand!" He caught back his temper with an effort. "I just gave you money before you left Los Angeles. How could you possibly have spent all of it? What do you do? Give it away?"

LaRaine dropped all pretense of blithe unconcern. "I didn't call to hear you lecture me about money. Can you advance me the money or not?" If he didn't, she didn't have the slightest idea where she would get it.

"You realize that if I do, the money you're receiving for this film will have already been spent. You won't have any more coming."

"Yes, I realize that," she admitted curtly.

"Very well, I'll transfer the money into your account, but don't call me for another cent," Peter warned.

"But darling," she stressed the endearment with cloying sweetness, "you are my agent. Who else would I call?"

"Don't remind me." The line went dead as he hung up.

Biting her lip, she stared at the phone before finally placing it back in its cradle. She glanced at the bank statement with its overdrawn notice and the bills scattered on the bed. The money wouldn't last very long. Peter was right; she really should be more careful with her money. But she had never had to pay attention to prices and budgets. They were completely alien to her.

"You just can't teach an old dog new tricks," LaRaine sighed aloud. "I simply have to marry someone with money. And soon!"

WITH THE CRISIS weathered, it was only a few days before she forgot all about it. Her financial straits crossed her mind fleetingly once when she bought a new dress for the party. She rationalized the purchase by convincing herself it might be the last new dress she could afford for a long time.

It was a beautiful red thing with a scooped neckline and long sleeves. The material was feather light, softly draping her figure. This scarlet shade of red was the perfect color to accent her brunette hair and flashing dark eyes. LaRaine applied a matching shade of red lipstick to her mouth with a brush, carefully outlining the curves and then filling them in.

There was a knock at her door. LaRaine set the lipbrush down and went to answer it. Travis stood in the hallway. Wearing a cream tan sports jacket that molded the breadth of his shoulders and tapered to his waist, he looked casual and ruggedly handsome.

"I'll be ready in a minute." LaRaine stepped out of the doorway. "Come in and sit down."

His dark gaze skimmed her from head to toe, then reversed its course. "You look fine."

"Give me a few minutes and I'll look better," she promised. She liked the way the dress swirled silently around her legs as she turned to walk back to the vanity mirror. "I'm sorry the accommodations don't include an in-room bar or I'd offer you a drink while you're waiting."

"That's all right."

Instead of sitting on the one lone chair in the room, Travis followed her to the mirror. Unbuttoning his jacket, he slipped his hands into the pockets of his brown pants and leaned a shoulder against the wall to watch her.

Usually LaRaine was indifferent to people watching her, including men, but Travis's study made her uneasy. With the red applied to every centimeter of her lips, she powdered them, blotted that off with a damp cosmetic sponge and added gloss. Her hand trembled slightly as she penciled short, feathery lines to increase the fullness of her naturally arching eyebrows.

She was grateful she had already applied her makeup base and the various makeup coloring sticks to contour her face. A subtle blend of three eyeshadows covered her lids as well as a discreet amount of charcoal eyeliner. A half-dozen coats of mascara made her lashes longer and thicker than normal. She had spent almost an hour on her hair. If Travis had watched her doing that, she doubted that she would have achieved this perfect effect.

Before she was completely satisfied, LaRaine added a touch more blusher to her cheekbones. She studied the result in the mirror, then glanced at Travis.

"How do I look?" she asked, knowing the answer couldn't be anything but positive.

A slow smile spread across his strong mouth. "Fine." Which was the same thing he had said before.

There was something about his expression that LaRaine didn't like. "Why are you smiling?" It was a half-demanding and half-laughing question.

"I was trying to decide whether I was looking at a little girl playing 'grown-up' with her mommy's lipstick or a grown woman hiding from the world behind a painted mask." Travis continued to watch her reaction with lazy interest.

His answer made LaRaine study her reflection in the mirror. It implied that something was wrong. But she couldn't see anywhere where she had been heavy-handed with the makeup.

"What's wrong?" Her dark eyes were wide and confused. "Don't you think I look beautiful?"

"Yes, you look beautiful." Travis agreed on one hand, and took it back with the other. "Like the photograph of some fashion model. So perfect that you don't look real. Everybody else has moles while models have beauty marks."

LaRaine was irritated. "Isn't that just like a man?" she demanded of no one. "I spend hours getting ready, styling my hair and putting on my makeup just to look beautiful to you. And what's your reaction? You accuse me of not looking real or being a little girl playing with lipstick."

"Why did you leave out a woman hiding behind a painted mask?" he queried, alertly catching her omission. "Do you wear all that makeup so people can't see how scared you are inside?"

LaRaine pushed away from the table. "I've never heard anything so ridiculous in all my life! I wear makeup for the same reason that every other woman does—because I want to look my best." Rising to her feet, she walked to the door and paused when Travis didn't follow her. "Are you ready to go?" she demanded impatiently.

Travis straightened from the wall. "I thought you might want to wait a bit longer before you make your entrance at the party."

"In another minute I might change my mind and decide not to go at all." The fuse of her temper was sparking with fire.

"We can't have that happen." With long, easy strides, Travis crossed the room to open the door for her. "Everyone might think you were lying when you said I was bringing you to the party if we didn't show up."

It was an unwelcome reminder of the ploy she had

used to obtain his agreement. LaRaine pressed her lips tightly closed, not making any reply to his mocking words. His hand was at her back to guide her down the hallway to the hotel exit. The body heat emanating from his touch seemed to burn through the thin material of her dress. She was rigidly conscious of his brawny frame, tall and rugged, shortening his strides to match hers. She felt small, and not just because his height emphasized her petite build.

How had this happened, she demanded of herself as he walked her into the parking lot. She had handled him so easily the other day when they'd been riding. Everything had gone so well. Why was he taunting her now, saying all those things about her?

When they approached the entrance to the private hall that had been rented for the party, she felt Travis looking at her, but she wouldn't glance at him. She would show him. No one treated her like that and got away with it.

"Are you going to pout all night?" His low voice prodded, making her conscious of the faintly jutting line of her lower lip.

"I am not pouting," she retorted.

"I hurt your feelings, didn't I?" His question was mixed with curiosity and amusement.

"Nothing you could say could possibly hurt my feelings," LaRaine flashed, striking back by attacking how unimportant she considered him to be.

His mouth curved in a complacent smile that mocked her assertion as Travis reached in front of her to open the door. LaRaine fumed silently, but this was not the time to be trading angry words. Inside the party was in full swing. The music from a tape deck blared through the long room; its pulsing beat filled the air.

As party members glanced around to see who had arrived, LaRaine linked her arm with Travis's and smiled as if she hadn't a care in the world. She guessed how hypocritical he would regard her action when, not two seconds ago, she had been snapping at him.

They made their way across the room toward the makeshift bar in the corner, with LaRaine laughing and calling out greetings. She knew what she was doing. She was showing off, making certain everyone saw her with Travis. Vivacious and bubbling, she clung to his arm, laughing up at him but avoiding direct contact with his gaze.

There was a cluster of people at the bar. Most of them already had drinks in their hands and were just standing around talking.

"What would you like to drink?" Travis asked.

"Whatever you're having, darling," LaRaine answered, loud enough for everyone to hear.

Travis turned to one of the crew who was acting as bartender and ordered, "Two beers."

A cast member was leaning against the bar. When he heard the subsequent order, he hooted, "Beer! I thought you never drank anything but champagne cocktails, LaRaine." He laughed and everyone around joined in.

She loathed and despised beer. "Whoever told you that, Mike?" She laughed in denial, and lied, "I like beer."

"If you'd wanted something else, you should have asked for it," Travis told her quietly, a cool challenge in his look as he pressed a cold can of beer in her gesturing hand.

"This is fine," she insisted with false brightness, and tried not to gag when she took a sip from the can.

It was dreadful; she knew she would never be able to drink it all. She had to find a diversion. A new rock tune began to play. LaRaine set the can on the bar and reached for Travis's hand.

"Let's dance," she urged.

"No, I don't dance," he refused.

"It's easy. I'll teach you." Tipping her head to one side, she looked up at him through the alluring sweep of her long lashes and gave him a coaxing smile.

"No." He was unmoved by her charming attempt at persuasion. "If you want to dance, you'll have to find someone else."

His absolute indifference to the embarrassment he was causing her by rejecting her invitation in front of everyone infuriated her. She cast aside her mask of gaiety.

"Do you think I can't?" she hissed for his hearing alone. His dark brow arched briefly in unconcern. She whirled away from him, her skirt billowing like a shimmering red cloud. She fixed her gaze on the nearest man. "Dance with me, Mike," she ordered, and took the drink from his hand, setting it beside hers on the bar.

He was trying to protest as she led him to a cleared area of the room where there were others dancing. Once there he gave in and began moving with the driving rhythm. LaRaine cast a smug look in Travis's direction, but he wasn't paying any attention to her.

Angered again, she centered all her interest on her dancing partner, smiling and flirting with him outrageously to obtain her revenge.

When the song ended, Mike pleaded exhaustion. LaRaine started to walk back to the bar with him. The sight of Travis, his dark head bent attentively toward the tall blonde from Wardrobe, made her change direction. She snared another unattached male cast member and dragged him onto the dance floor for the next song.

After that song he was still with the blonde. They had been joined by Susan, another girl from Wardrobe, and one of the stunt men. LaRaine found another partner. It went on and on like that. She kept waiting for Travis to claim her in between dances, but it was as if he had forgotten all about her; as if she never existed and he had never brought her to the party at all. Beneath her raging anger she was close to tears.

Her temper carried her through three more dances. LaRaine stopped looking to see where Travis was or who he was with, ignoring him the same way he was ignoring her. Finally she ran out of partners and was forced to leave the floor. She glanced around the room for Travis, intending to boast falsely about how much fun she was having and subtly let him know that the way he had been ignoring her hadn't hurt one bit.

There was no sign of him in her first sweep of the room. LaRaine looked again, wondering how she had missed him. Travis was so tall and stood out so from the others that she had been able to spot him instantly all the previous times. A tiny frown creased her forehead when her second search was equally unsuccessful.

Working her way around the crowded room, La-Raine continued to look for him. A painful suspicion was beginning to form in her mind. Then she saw Susan talking to the tall blonde Travis had been with earlier. If he hadn't gone somewhere with either of them, where was he? Her frown of uncertainty deepened.

"Looking for someone?" Sam Hardesty was at her elbow.

LaRaine erased the frown from her expression and forced a bright smile. "Travis. Have you seen him?"

"He's gone home, back to the ranch," he told her, swaying unsteadily and lifting the drink in his hand to his mouth.

She laughed off his answer. "Will you stop trying to be funny, Sam? Have you seen him or not?"

"I'm not joking, LaRaine." He shook his head and smiled, taking delight in the frozen look stealing over her face. "He said to tell you he'd had enough."

"Do you mean he just walked out and left me here?" she demanded. Humiliation burned through her veins, coloring her ivory skin. "He can't do that!"

"He did. He's gone." Sam continued to smile with satisfaction. "Look around for yourself. You've already done that, though, haven't you?" he mocked.

LaRaine was trembling, vibrating in outrage and mortification. "He isn't going to get away with this!"

Her teeth were clenched to keep her chin from quivering. "Let me borrow your car, Sam." When he hesitated, she added a taut, "Please."

"Sure." Sam fumbled through his pocket and handed her the keys. "It's the burgundy Continental parked at the corner."

Just for a second LaRaine let herself be sidetracked by his announcement. "Continental?" He'd been driving a late model Ford the last she knew.

"Yeah, brand new." There was an unnatural glitter in his eyes. "Maybe you shouldn't have been so quick to turn me down."

She hesitated, then replied, "If you had a million dollars, I think I would have turned *you* down."

She suspected that she just might be telling the truth. In more rational moments it might have been a shocking discovery, but right now she was too obsessed with going after Travis.

CHAPTER SIX

THE POWERFUL CAR sped out of town onto the main highway. A full moon bathed the rough countryside with silver light. LaRaine's foot was heavy on the accelerator as she raced the car through the night. She almost missed the unmarked gate and the dirt road leading back to the ranchyard.

Making the turn, she drove as fast as she dared over the winding track. On a curve, her headlight beams briefly caught the glowing eyes of a wild animal before it slunk away into the darkness. It didn't arouse her interest. Her only thought was of Travis and the things she intended to say to him.

It seemed to take forever before she crested the rise and saw the dark outlines of the ranch buildings silhouetted against the moonlit sky. There was a light on in the house. LaRaine stepped on the gas to speed over the last hundred yards. The tires skidded and slipped as she braked to a halt in front of the house.

A dog came racing out of the barn to bark at the intruder. LaRaine ignored it as she stormed out of the car and onto the porch. Not bothering to knock, she jerked open the door and sailed into the house. Travis was halfway across the living room, wearing the same brown slacks. His cream shirt was completely unbuttoned and hanging open. He stopped; his gaze narrowed at the sight of LaRaine sweeping toward him.

"How dare you treat me like that!" She confronted him, her hands doubled into fists held rigidly at her side. "How dare you walk out and leave me! Nobody treats me like that!"

"Maybe it was time somebody did." Travis didn't raise his voice to meet the angry pitch of hers, but kept it calmly reasonable and cool.

Her hand lashed out to strike at his cheek. With lightning reflexes, Travis caught her wrist, his strong fingers completely circling its slenderness. LaRaine strained to pull her wrist free of his hold, but it was no use.

"I was never so humiliated in all my life!" she stormed. "I had to find out from Sam that you'd left— you didn't even have the decency to tell me yourself."

"I warned you that I wouldn't be used." His eyes narrowed into coal-black slits. "You asked me to take you to that party to save your precious pride. I did. Five minutes after we walked through the door, you went off on your own to have fun with your friends."

"You weren't exactly bored while I was gone," LaRaine accused. "I saw you talking to Karen, from Wardrobe, and Susan. You weren't interested in where I was or what I was doing."

"Did you expect me to go off in a corner and sulk because you weren't with me?" The sardonic line of his mouth quirked to show her how ludicrous that thought was.

"I didn't expect you to go off and leave me there by myself!" she flashed in resentment. "I thought you were a gentleman. Obviously I was wrong."

"It's funny you should make that mistake." There was the hard glitter of amusement in his look. "I guessed all along that you weren't a lady."

Stung by his insult, LaRaine raised her free hand, nails curled to claw at his face. It was as easily captured as the first. When she attempted to struggle, she was hauled roughly against his chest, her arms twisted behind her back to make her a helpless captive. Her raven-black hair swung about her shoulders as she tipped her head back to glare at him.

"You dirty rotten b—"

His mouth crushed down on her lips, making her eat the curses she longed to hurl at him. With his shirt opened, she was arched against his naked chest. Wiry, dark hairs scraped her bare skin above the scooped neckline of her dress. His fiery body heat seemed to burn right through the thin material to envelop her in its blazing warmth.

Smothered, LaRaine couldn't seem to catch her breath. Everything seemed to be reeling. The bruising force of his kiss had bent her head back so far that she thought her neck would snap. She had been drawn into the vortex of his anger, and realized that she wasn't all that eager to escape the spinning madness of his arms.

A series of thudding sounds penetrated her consciousness. At first LaRaine thought it was the drumming of her heart. When a knock rattled the screen door, she realized what she had heard were footsteps on the wooden floor of the porch. His mouth ended its crushing possession of hers as her arms were untwisted from behind her back, but Travis kept hold of her. His expressionless face was turned toward the door. La-

Raine took a shaky breath and tried to fight free of the haze that enveloped her senses.

The screen door rattled again. "Travis?" a young male voice called. "Is there anything wrong? I heard the car and—"

"Nothing's wrong, Joe," Travis answered.

LaRaine was amazed at how quickly he controlled his anger to sound calm and unruffled. Of course, the punishing kiss had driven out her own anger, so maybe it had worked the same for him, providing a release.

There was hesitation from the porch, then the thud of footsteps on the boards. LaRaine's pulse had still not settled down to its normal rate when the footsteps could no longer be heard. She stared at the curling hairs darkening Travis's chest, not ready yet to meet his gaze.

"Who was that?" she murmured.

"My hired hand."

"Where was he?" It seemed easier to talk about him.

"He sleeps in the shed," Travis answered.

"In the shed? That broken-down old building near the barn?" LaRaine couldn't believe it was the one he meant.

"It's sturdier than it looks," he informed her dryly. He turned her around and pointed her toward the door.

"What are you doing?" she protested.

"You're leaving," Travis stated, and marched her to the door.

"What if I'm not ready to go?" LaRaine challenged, pulling back.

"This happens to be my home," he reminded her. Opening the door, he pushed her onto the porch. "I didn't invite you here. You just barged in."

"And now you're telling me to get out," she concluded tightly. His hand on her elbow kept her from tripping down the porch steps.

"You could put it that way," Travis agreed, and walked her to the car as if he wanted to make certain she left.

"Why don't you ride with me as far as the highway?" LaRaine challenged sarcastically. "That way you can make sure that I'm off your property."

He opened the car door and pushed her inside behind the wheel. Holding the door open, he looked down at the rebellion flashing in her eyes.

"You're a spoiled, selfish little brat," he said flatly. "You want everything your way and you don't care who you hurt getting it. Life doesn't work that way, and it's time you learned that. I hope tonight was the first of many lessons."

He slammed the door shut without giving her a chance to respond to his accusations. LaRaine shivered at the freezing scorn that had been in his voice. Tears burned her eyes, but she kept them at bay as she turned the ignition key. The front fender of the luxury car narrowly missed grazing Travis as she made a sharp turn to take the dirt road back to the highway. Once she had left the tall man behind, tears streamed down her cheeks. She kept wiping them away, but it only seemed to make room for more.

She drove recklessly back to town, speeding, half the time blinded by tears. She kept telling herself that she didn't know why she was crying and that she didn't care a snap about his opinion of her.

The parking space on the corner was still empty, although LaRaine noticed that the space right behind it was occupied by a highway patrol car. She sniffed and wiped the tears from her face one last time as she carefully parked the Continental in the same spot she had taken it from. The last person she wanted to face was Sam, so she left the keys in the car rather than give them back to him in person.

As she climbed out of the car, she noticed that the patrolman behind her did also. She was certain she hadn't done anything illegal. She ignored him and started to walk to the hotel.

"Wait a minute, miss." It was unmistakably an order.

She hesitated, then stopped. After all that crying, she probably looked a mess, but there was nothing she could do about repairing her makeup now. Gathering all her poise, she turned.

"What is it, officer?" she demanded.

A rotund figure was puffing after the approaching patrolman. When he recognized LaRaine, he stopped short beneath a streetlight and his face turned twenty shades of red.

"You!" he sputtered finally. "You're the one who stole my car?"

"Your car?" LaRaine repeated, staring at the director with a sinking heart. "But I thou—"

"Do you know this woman?" the patrolman asked Andrew Behr.

"Unfortunately, yes," he said as he expelled an angry sigh. "She's an actress, a lousy actress."

Her feet seemed to be rooted to the pavement. It hadn't been Sam's car. It belonged to the director, yet Sam had let her believe it was his. He had given her the keys. Now she was being accused of stealing it.

"You weren't aware that she'd taken your car?" the uniformed officer questioned.

"No," the director denied, glaring at her. "I came out here to get in my car and it was gone. If she took it, it was without my permission."

"But—" LaRaine began weakly, only to be drowned out by the patrolman.

"Did you leave your keys in the car?"

"I told you I don't remember," Andrew Behr answered impatiently. "I might have."

Light flashed from the building behind the two men as a door was opened and closed. LaRaine noticed a man standing in the shadows of the overhang. It took her a second to recognize Sam. She took a step forward to ask him to explain to the officer and the director that he had loaned her the car. Then she realized that he would deny it. He had done it deliberately, hoping to get her into trouble. He had succeeded.

"Do you wish to press charges against her?" the patrolman asked. "You do have the car back. There doesn't seem to be any damage to it."

LaRaine spoke up in her own defense. "I didn't steal the car—I borrowed it."

The director paused before answering the patrolman. He seemed to do it deliberately to let LaRaine dangle over the heat of the fire, hoping she would cry out for mercy.

"No," be said finally, his voice ominously low.

"No, I won't press charges. I'll handle this my own way. I'm sorry to have troubled you."

"That's what I'm paid for." The patrolman touched his hat in a one-fingered salute before returning to his marked car.

Andrew Behr walked to the middle of the street where LaRaine stood. She offered no apologies or explanations; she knew she would be wasting her breath. When he reached her side, they walked in unison to the sidewalk.

"Shall I say it?" he asked when they stopped at the other side.

"You might as well," LaRaine answered brazenly. "If nothing else, then just to make it official."

"You're through, finished!" he snapped. "I don't want to see you or hear from you again. I want you packed and gone in the morning."

"By morning?" she smiled sweetly. "I'm surprised you're giving me that long."

"Keep that up and I might change my mind," he threatened.

"Excuse me." LaRaine kept the saccharine smile in place. "I have a lot of packing to do."

Turning her back on the man, she walked to the hotel, not stopping until she reached her room. She walked to the vanity table and sank into the chair. Staring at her reflection in the mirror, she noticed that other than her mascara being smudged, her face was unravaged by the tears she'd cried. Numbly she set about repairing the slight damage.

Halfway through, she began laughing. The world had fallen in around her head and she was fixing her makeup. She realized she was on the verge of hysteria and sobered. What was she going to do?

She walked to where she had left her purse and counted out her money. She sank onto the bed in numbed shock. Where had it all gone? There was barely more than twenty dollars in her billfold. Most of it had gone to pay bills and cover her overdrawn account, she realized. The rest she had squandered on the red dress she was wearing. She remembered her agent's lecture and wished she had paid more heed to it.

Hope flickered briefly. Maybe Peter would loan her some more money. No—LaRaine shook her head. The minute he learned she had been fired, he would probably wash his hands of her. Her parents? She had had a postcard from them a week ago. They were vacationing somewhere, a long ocean cruise, LaRaine thought, but she couldn't remember where and she'd thrown the card away.

There was a knock at her door. LaRaine ignored it, hoping whoever it was would go away. But the knocking persisted. She scooped up the contents of her purse and dumped them back in the bag. After running a smoothing hand over the midnight black of her hair, she walked to the door and opened it.

Sam was leaning against the door jamb, a knowing smile on his face. "Hi, LaRaine. I thought I might find you here."

There was a faint slur in his voice, but he looked more sober than he had at the party. For a minute LaRaine toyed with the idea of asking him for help, but something in his expression told her that was what he was waiting for. He wanted the revenge of turning her down, the way she had rejected him. She wouldn't give him the satisfaction.

"What do you want, Sam?" she demanded instead.

"The old man kicked you out, didn't he?" His mouth twisted into a cruel smile.

"If you've come to gloat, you're wasting your time." LaRaine walked away from the door. "I've had it with this place. I'm glad I don't have to stay around here any longer."

He followed her into the room and closed the door. "You wanted the job bad enough a couple of months ago," he reminded her.

"Things change. People change." She shrugged. "Look at you—good, kind, sweet Sam. This was all your doing. You set me up deliberately. You gave me the keys, let me believe it was your car, and probably told Behr it was gone."

"I did warn you not to cross him," Sam told her.

"Then you arranged to make sure that I did, didn't you?" LaRaine challenged.

"I guess I did, didn't I?" he admitted.

"I know you regret that you helped me get this job," she said. "But I would have had a lot more respect for you, Sam, if you'd had the guts to fire me yourself instead of tricking someone else into doing the dirty work for you. You've just given me one more reason why I'm glad I never agreed to marry you."

"Is that right?" He seemed not in the least disturbed by her denouncement of him.

"Yes, that's right." Spinning on her heel, LaRaine walked to the vanity table where she picked up a brush and began running it through her hair.

"So you think it was a mean, dirty trick I played on you?" Sam questioned.

Her hair crackled with electricity. LaRaine felt charged by it, too. "It was," she snapped.

"You've done it all your life," he accused. "You tricked your cousin into impersonating you so you could make your first movie without Montgomery ever discovering it. Later I heard about the way you tried to trick Corbett's girl friend into believing you and Corbett were having an affair. You've tricked others, more successfully. I was one of them."

"You're a sore loser, Sam." LaRaine set the brush down and fluffed her raven hair with her fingers, pretending a total indifference to his words.

"No, I'm a wise one. And I just hope that after tonight you know what it's like to be a victim of a dirty trick. It's a painful experience to go sailing along and have someone pull the rug out from underneath you when you're not looking."

Her natural ivory complexion grew whiter as Sam explained his motivation. He knew just how harshly he had brought her down, because he knew how badly she had needed this job. He studied her stricken look with satisfaction.

"I hope it hurts, LaRaine," he said. "You've always wanted to believe that you belonged on a pedestal. Well, you don't." He walked to the door, opened it and paused. "I won't wish you good luck. I'll save it for the next poor sucker you find."

With the closing of the door, something inside LaRaine crumpled. She stared after him for several minutes. Then mechanically, she began undressing and changing into her filmy nightgown. Crawling into bed, she stared at the ceiling. Sam's words kept mixing with what Travis had told her—that he hoped tonight would be the first of many lessons. It was a long, long time before she slept.

A knock on her door wakened her the next morning. LaRaine didn't want to wake up, preferring the oblivion of sleep to the problems she faced. She pulled the pillow over her head to try to shut out the persistent knocking.

Finally, groggy from sleep that had brought her no rest, she climbed out of bed and tugged on the matching robe to complete her negligee set. Not bothering to tie the robe closed, she held it shut with her hand. She walked to the door and opened it a crack to look bleary-eyed at the desk manager of the hotel.

"I've been told you're leaving this morning," he said. "I wondered what time you intend to vacate the room?"

LaRaine ran a hand across her eyes and tried to think. If she left, where would she go? But she had to leave. Even disregarding Andrew Behr's orders for her to be packed and gone, she didn't have the money to pay for a hotel room.

"I...I haven't packed yet," she stalled. Which was true. "As a matter of fact, you just woke me up."

The manager didn't apologize for that. LaRaine could well imagine what the director had probably told the man about her. She didn't have a chance of appealing to the manager to let her stay another day.

"Twelve noon should give you sufficient time to pack your things," he told her.

"Noon, yes, that will be fine." She smiled wanly. What else could she say?

The man nodded curtly and turned to walk down the hallway toward the lobby. LaRaine closed the door and leaned her shoulder against it. The room was a mess, clothes scattered everywhere. And she was supposed to pack and be out of the room by noon.

Sighing heavily, she walked to the bathroom. First things came first. She would shower, get dressed, put on her makeup, then pack. If she were a few minutes late, then it was just their tough luck.

The shower did her a world of good. She felt refreshed, more able to battle whatever was to come. Going through her crowded closet, she selected her outfit with care—a faded pair of tight-fitting jeans and a yellow knit T-shirt. It was simple, down-to-earth, and exactly the image she wanted to portray.

Next came the makeup. The base and contouring color sticks were standard routine. But LaRaine used less eyeshadow and chose a tawny combination of shades with a light usage of brown eyeliner. The mascara, too, she was careful not to overuse. Instead of red lipstick, she applied a more natural color that tinted her lips. Brushing her raven hair until it glistened, she let it swing free about her shoulders, its style loose and casual.

The hard part was next—packing. The closet was jammed with clothes and so was the dresser. Outside of weekend trips, LaRaine had never done any major packing in her life. There had always been someone else to do it—a maid or her mother or her cousin.

Dragging the suitcases out of the closet, she opened

them on the bed. Without following any natural order, she began folding garments and laying them in the cases. She ran out of room before she ran out of clothes. Her brief attempt at neatness was abandoned as she began cramming clothes and cosmetics into any and every available hole.

Closing and locking them became the next problem, solved when she sat on them. It took all her strength to drag the bigger cases off the bed and set them on the floor. Normally LaRaine would have called to have a porter carry her luggage to the lobby, but that would mean tipping. The few dollars she had could be better spent on other things.

It took her three trips before all her luggage was sitting in the hotel lobby. Her arms ached with the effort. She glanced at the clock above the desk. It was half past eleven. She had made the deadline, she thought triumphantly.

The manager was sitting at the switchboard behind the counter. LaRaine walked to it and dropped her key on the top. He turned at the sound. His gaze flicked past her to the suitcases she had piled near the door.

"All packed, I see," he commented.

"Yes," she nodded. "I was wondering if you knew of someone I might hire to drive me where I want to go."

"How far were you going?" he questioned. "The bus stop is just a few blocks—"

"I'm not going to the bus station," LaRaine informed him. She didn't have the price of a ticket to Los Angeles.

"Where, then?" he frowned.

There was only one place she could go and one person who might help her. None of the cast or crew would assist her. LaRaine knew that without asking. Once she would have believed that Sam might have, but after last night she knew better.

"The McCrea ranch, outside of town," she answered.

CHAPTER SEVEN

LaRaine held on tightly as the old pickup truck bounced over the dirt road to the ranch. She was afraid to look through the back window at her expensive leather suitcases sliding from side to side in the rusty bed of the truck. The crusty old man behind the wheel seemed to have a death wish, considering the speed he was driving over the road. It was no wonder the springs no longer could absorb the shock of the ruts and chuckholes. It was a worse ride than the one Sam had made over the same road.

As they crested the rise and the ranch buildings came into sight clustered on the mesa, LaRaine almost sighed aloud in relief that they had made it in one piece. The man hadn't said two words to her the entire trip. Not that she particularly wanted to talk. Neither did she want to think.

"Don't look like no one's home," the old man observed as the truck hiccuped to a stop in front of the house.

"That's all right. I'll wait," LaRaine told him, and climbed shakily out of the cab of the truck.

The door didn't want to close. "I'll get that. There's a trick to it," he informed her, and walked over to kick the door shut with his boot.

GET 4 BOOKS

FREE

Return this card, and we'll send you 4 brand-new Harlequin Presents® novels, absolutely *FREE!* We'll even pay the postage both ways!

We're making you this offer to introduce you to the benefits of the Harlequin Reader Service®: free home delivery of brand-new romance novels, months before they're available in stores, **AND** at a saving of 40¢ apiece compared to the cover price!

Accepting these 4 free books places you under no obligation to continue. You may cancel at any time, even just after receiving your free shipment. If you do not cancel, every month we'll send 6 more Harlequin Presents novels and bill you just $2.49* apiece—that's all!

Yes! Please send me my 4 free Harlequin Presents novels, as explained above.

Name

Address   Apt.

City   State   Zip

106 CIH AGPA (U-JDA-11/92)

*Terms and prices subject to change without notice. Sales tax applicable in NY. Offer limited to one per household and not valid to current Harlequin Presents subscribers. All orders subject to approval.   © 1990 Harlequin Enterprises Limited.

Printed in Canada

DETACH ALONG DOTTED LINE AND MAIL TODAY! – DETACH ALONG DOTTED LINE AND MAIL TODAY! – DETACH ALONG DOTTED LINE AND MAIL TODAY! – DETACH ALONG DOTTED LINE AND MAIL TODAY!

Get 4 Books FREE
SEE BACK OF CARD FOR DETAILS

FREE MYSTERY GIFT

We will be happy to send you a free bonus gift along with your free books! To request it, please check here and mail this reply card promptly!

Thank you!

BUSINESS REPLY CARD
FIRST CLASS MAIL   PERMIT NO. 717   BUFFALO, NY

POSTAGE WILL BE PAID BY ADDRESSEE

HARLEQUIN READER SERVICE®
3010 WALDEN AVE
P O BOX 1867
BUFFALO NY 14240-9952

NO POSTAGE
NECESSARY
IF MAILED
IN THE
UNITED STATES

DETACH ALONG DOTTED LINE AND MAIL TODAY! – DETACH ALONG DOTTED LINE AND MAIL TODAY! – DETACH ALONG DOTTED LINE AND MAIL TODAY!

"The trick is sheer brute force." LaRaine shrugged.

"But only if you kick it in the right place." Moving to the rear of the truck, he began dragging her suitcases to the tailgate.

"Please be careful with them!" She winced at the treatment he was giving them. There were already scratches on the sides. But he paid no more attention to her now than when he had loaded them in the truck. He stacked them on the ground.

When they were all out, he turned to her and held out his hand. "We agreed on five dollars."

"Yes." She opened up her purse and took out the bill. "Thank you." She gave it to him.

"You're welcome." He tipped his hat and walked back to the truck.

It backfired as he started back up the dirt road. The chickens scratching in the yard scattered in a blur of dust and flying feathers. LaRaine coughed and waved a hand to clear the air in front of her.

Glancing at the suitcases piled on the ground, she wished she had asked him to carry them to the porch. He would probably have charged her extra, she thought wryly. Picking up the largest with both hands, she lugged it to the porch.

When all of them were on the porch, she sat down on the strongest of them all to wait for Travis. She had briefly contemplated going into the house where she would be out of the dust and sun, but she remembered Travis's reaction when she had walked in uninvited the last time. She needed his help desperately; she could not risk offending him.

Directly overhead the sun grew hotter and hotter.

LaRaine wished for a drink of cold, cold water. Then the sound of cantering hooves made her forget the thirst. Rising quickly to her feet she walked to the corner of the porch and shaded her eyes. Two riders were coming in. One was Travis and the second had to be his hired hand.

Her hand was resting against the corner post, tension running through her nerve ends stringing them taut. The riders were approaching the rear of the barn, which kept them from having a clear view of the house.

Then LaRaine saw Travis slow his horse and change its angle so he could see the house. She guessed that he had caught a glimpse of her. She waved, wanting desperately to speak to him alone. It would be embarrassing if she had to tell her story in front of the young hired man.

She heard Travis call something to the other rider, but the distance made the words indistinguishable. Reining his horse away from the barn, he guided it directly to the house. The bay horse trotted into the yard, slowing to a stop in front of the porch.

Studying his rugged features, LaRaine tried to find a clue to his reaction to finding her there, but his expression was unreadable. His dark gaze raked her, then slashed to the suitcases stacked on his porch.

"What are you doing here?" he asked in a quiet voice.

LaRaine felt pinned by his thrusting gaze. "I'm in trouble, Travis."

He hooked his right leg across the saddle horn and leaned on it. She realized he was waiting for an explanation of that statement. Moistening her dry lips she completely forgot her rehearsed speech, blowing her lines as she had done so often in front of the camera.

"I was fired," she admitted. "I lost my job and was evicted from the hotel."

"Why?" Just the one word.

"Because—" LaRaine took a deep breath "—the car I drove here in last night belonged to the director. I thought it was Sam's. He gave me the keys, but he didn't tell Mr. Behr. When I got back to town last night, Behr was notifying the police that someone had stolen his car—me. He didn't have me arrested, but he fired me and ordered me to pack up and leave."

"Sam didn't explain?"

"No." She laughed shortly and without humor. "Do you remember what you said last night about the lessons I needed to learn? Well, Sam gave me lesson number two. So I would know what it felt like to be tricked."

"None of this explains why you're here," Travis stated.

"I'm broke. All I had was twenty dollars, and I had to give five of it to the man who drove me out here. I couldn't think of anyone who might help me." Her voice cracked on the last, the desperateness of her situation creeping through.

"What makes you think I'd help you?" He eyed her narrowly, not moving out of his relaxed pose, leaning on the knee hooked around the saddle horn. Yet he was alert, unnervingly so.

"Because I—" LaRaine faltered "—I remembered

what you said about being an easy prey for women in trouble."

She saw the silent laugh Travis breathed out before he looked away and shook his head. His dark eyes glittered with sardonic amusement when they refocused on her. The line of his mouth was hard and unrelenting.

"So you expect me to give you some money," he drawled in a voice that didn't admit whether he would or not.

"Yes." LaRaine held her breath.

"How much do you need?" The bay horse stamped at a fly and the saddle creaked beneath Travis as his mount shifted.

That sounded very positive. She moistened her lips, hardly daring to hope. "I could use a thousand." At the lift of his eyebrow, she added hastily, "But I could get by with five hundred."

Travis studied the reins held loosely in a leather-gloved hand. "You're asking me to give you five hundred."

"I'll pay you back," LaRaine promised.

"I have a feeling I'd have to wait a long time." His mouth crooked cynically.

"I'll pay you back as soon as I can. You have my word on that." But the glint in his eye said he didn't put much stock in her word. She had built her hopes up so high and Travis had let her. Stung by his mocking attitude, LaRaine challenged, "Will you give me the money?"

"No."

It was a flat denial without qualification. Her eyes smarted and she pivoted away to face the wild land spreading out from the ranch buildings. She blinked furiously at the moisture in her eyes, not wanting Travis to see how close she was to crying. Where would she go now? What would she do? She didn't even have a place to sleep tonight.

"I know how you might earn the money you need," Travis told her, "if you're willing to work."

"Where?" She spun around, grasping at any straw.

"Here, for me." He watched her closely.

"What do I have to do? How much would you pay?" she rushed.

"I'll pay you fifty dollars a week plus room and board to take care of the house."

"Fifty dollars?" LaRaine repeated incredulously. It was such a paltry sum, a tenth of what she needed.

"Plus room and board," Travis reminded her dryly.

"But it would take me ten weeks to earn enough money to leave here," she protested. "Why won't you just give me the money?"

"Because I can't afford to give away the money without getting something in return for it."

"But fifty dollars?" LaRaine repeated again, and looked about her before turning her imploring brown eyes on Travis. "Why can't you pay me a hundred dollars a week?"

Travis tilted his head to one side. "You came to me for help. Fifty dollars a week is my offer. Take it or leave it," he answered.

Her jaw was clenched as she met his unwavering gaze. "What's this? Another lesson?" she challenged bitterly.

"From your viewpoint, it probably is. From mine—"

Travis paused "—I'm paying wages to a housekeeper so that I can devote my time completely to running the ranch. What's your answer?"

"I don't have any choice." LaRaine glared at him resentfully. "I don't have any place to go, no place to sleep, and very little money. I'll take it."

Straightening, Travis unhooked his knee from the saddle horn and stepped down off the horse. He glanced at the barn and called, "Joe!"

A slim figure stepped out of the interior shadows. "Yes, sir?"

"Will you take care of the bay for me?" It was an order phrased as a request.

The hired hand trotted across the yard to obey. As he drew closer, the impression of youth increased. The chest and shoulders were just beginning to muscle out. There was a fresh, open quality about his features.

"Joe, this is Miss Evans," Travis introduced. "She's going to keep house for me." To LaRaine, he identified, "This is Joe Benteen."

"Hello, Joe." LaRaine attempted to sound pleasant, stifling the resentment she felt toward Travis.

"Ma'am." Joe briefly lifted his black hat, grayed with dust. The action exposed the unusual red blond shade of his hair. There was a hint of shyness in the hazel eyes, but his smile seemed natural. LaRaine remembered that he was only nineteen.

"When you're through in the barn, Joe, come to the house," Travis told him. "I'll be needing your help."

"Sure thing." He took the horse's reins from Travis and led it to the barn.

Walking onto the porch, Travis picked up the two

heaviest suitcases and glanced at LaRaine. "We might as well bring your things inside."

She picked up the lightest of the three remaining pieces and followed him into the house. Her nose wrinkled in distaste at the deplorably furnished living room. Travis didn't take the hallway that led to the kitchen and the closed staircase to the second floor. Crossing the living room, he walked to a door and opened it.

It was a bedroom, LaRaine discovered as she followed Travis through the doorway. She guessed that because there was a bed and a dresser and a closet. It was almost monklike, with no pictures on the drab green walls to relieve its severity. Travis set her luggage on the floor at the foot of the bed.

"You'll have to wait to unpack until I can get my things moved out to the shed," he told her.

"The shed?" she echoed.

"Yes, I'll be sleeping out there."

"But why? I mean, you don't have to. There are bedrooms upstairs, aren't there?" LaRaine frowned.

He studied her with amused patience. "I know it may seem to you that we're relatively isolated out here, but things have a way of getting around. When people learn that I've hired a young, beautiful actress to keep house for me, they're going to talk—especially if we're sleeping under the same roof."

"So what?" She lifted her shoulders in a shrug of bewilderment. "I'm used to people talking about me. It doesn't bother me. I don't care what they say."

"But I care what they say. They're my neighbors, and I want their respect and trust. So you see, it isn't your reputation I'm trying to protect." Travis smiled lazily. "It's mine." Turning, he added over his shoulder, "I'll bring in the rest of your luggage."

When he came back, he set the last two pieces of her luggage on the floor beside the others. "That's all of it," he said.

"Look," LaRaine began guiltily, "I'm sorry to be putting you out of your home this way. I really am."

"If you mean that, I'll stay here and Joe can move into one of the upstairs bedrooms, then you can sleep in the shed," Travis suggested.

Stunned, LaRaine could only look at him with horror. She couldn't imagine sleeping in that broken-down building—there were probably rats and mice all over the place. Then she saw the wicked glint in his eye and realized he was teasing.

"I don't think that was very funny," she muttered.

Travis chuckled and walked into the living room. LaRaine stayed in the bedroom, fighting to control her temper. She didn't like being the butt of a joke. Joe came. She heard Travis give him orders to bring down an army cot from an upstairs bedroom and take it to the shed.

When all that was done, the two of them exchanged the small dresser that had obviously been in the shed for a larger chest of drawers from upstairs. Then Travis emptied his things from the dresser drawers and closet in the bedroom to make room for LaRaine's. She was unpacking when he returned to the house.

"Do you want some lunch?" He paused in the doorway.

"No, thanks." LaRaine tried to restrict her eating to one meal a day to avoid unwanted pounds.

A few minutes later she heard the clatter of pots in the kitchen. After that came an appetizing aroma filtering into the bedroom. LaRaine steadfastly ignored it and continued unpacking. She heard the scrape of chair legs across the linoleum floor of the kitchen and the muffled voices of Travis and Joe as they sat down to eat.

She had one suitcase emptied when chair legs scraped again and there was the clink of silverware on plates. The screen door slammed and footsteps crossed the porch. But a second pair of footsteps approached the bedroom and she glanced up when Travis's brawny frame darkened the doorway.

"Do you want to leave that for a minute?" He nodded toward the second suitcase she had started to unpack. "I'll show you where everything is."

"Okay," she agreed, and tossed the blouse she was holding back in the case.

She trailed behind him into the kitchen. He walked to a cupboard and opened it. "In here is where I keep the canned goods. There's flour, sugar, and other staples in the cupboard by the stove," he explained. "The dishes are in the cupboards by the sink. The pots and pans are in the lower cupboards."

Her mouth slowly opened in stunned protest as the reason for his explanation began to register. But her throat seemed incapable of making a sound. Travis started toward a fully enclosed side porch off the kitchen.

"In addition to the refrigerator, there's a freezer on the porch where I keep meat," he said.

"Are you expecting *me* to cook?" LaRaine choked out the question.

Travis stopped and slowly turned to face her, a scowling smile on his tanned face. "You don't think I'm paying you fifty dollars a week to dust the furniture, sweep the floor, and wash a few clothes, do you? Of course I expect you to cook the meals."

"I can't cook," she protested.

"What do you mean, you can't cook?" His amusement was tinged with exasperation. "You're bound to have fixed yourself a meal sometime in your life."

"If you classify putting cold meat between two slices of bread as fixing a meal, then I have. Other than that, I haven't even boiled water for tea!" Her voice rose on a shrill note of panic.

"Then it's about time you learned to cook," Travis said, grim faced.

The way he was looking at her made LaRaine feel stupid for never learning how to cook. She glanced away, reddening with embarrassment. Instinctively she tried to defend herself.

"I'm going to marry a man who'll be wealthy enough to hire a chef, so it hasn't been necessary for me to know how," she retorted.

"In the meantime, if you want to eat, you have to cook," he stated.

LaRaine was looking anywhere but at him. She saw the dirty dishes stacked on the counter beside the sink and knew she had just found another chore.

"I suppose I have to do the dishes, too," she grumbled in resentment, and lifted her beautifully kept hands and manicured nails. "They'll be ruined!"

"I'm sure they'll survive a few dunkings in dish-water," Travis said dryly.

She remembered another thing he had said earlier. "And I have to wash clothes?"

"The washing machine is on the side porch." He indicated the door behind him where he had said the freezer was.

"And the clothes dryer?" LaRaine questioned.

His mouth twitched as if he wanted to smile and didn't think he dared. "Behind the house there are two poles with wires stretched between them. You hang the clothes on the wire and wait for nature to dry them."

"A clothesline?" Her dark eyes rounded.

"Then you do know what it's called." Mockery danced in his eyes.

"Yes, I do know what it's called," she snapped. "Haven't you heard of modern conveniences, like dish-washers and clothes dryers?" She glanced around the kitchen in disgust. "I'm surprised you even have running water." Suddenly she became still, realizing that she hadn't seen the bathroom. She looked warily at Travis. "You do have a bathroom? An indoor facility, I mean, not an outhouse with a stupid little crescent moon on the door?"

"Yes, there's a bathroom," Travis chuckled softly. "It's off the porch, complete with flush toilet."

"Thank goodness," LaRaine muttered to herself.

"You can explore around on your own after you're through unpacking. I have to get to work," he said. "Plan on having supper ready around sundown."

"What am I supposed to fix? And how?" She made an open-handed gesture of angry bewilderment.

Travis took a deep breath and walked to the refrigerator. He opened the door and pointed inside. "Do you see that package of meat on the second shelf? It's a roast." Closing the door, he walked to a lower cupboard near the stove and opened the door, bending down to remove an oblong pan. "You put the roast in here and put the pan in the oven with the cover on at about three-thirty. About an hour later, peel some potatoes, carrots and onions and add them to the same pan with the roast. Do you understand that?"

"I . . . think so," she nodded hesitantly.

"I hope so." This time it was Travis who muttered to himself. To her, he said, "I'll see you later," and exited by the back door via the side porch.

When he had gone, LaRaine looked around the kitchen and wondered what she had got herself into. But what other choice had she had? Oh, well, she shrugged her shoulders. She had warned Travis that she didn't know how to cook. If he was willing to suffer the consequences, she was willing to try. After a few catastrophes, he might be willing to give her the money to leave. There was always a bright spot in every dark day.

Returning to the bedroom, she resumed her unpacking. It was after three o'clock before she remembered Travis's instructions about the roast. She hurried to the kitchen and took the package of meat from the refrigerator. Unwrapping it, she put it in the roasting pan, set the lid on it, and carried it to the stove.

The gas stove looked like an antique. Opening the oven door, she slid the pan onto the baking shelf and closed the door. She realized that Travis had omitted to tell her how to operate it. She studied the dials. One had graduating temperatures listed on it. LaRaine turned it, and opened the oven door to see if anything happened. Nothing. She tried each of the dials in turn and nothing happened. Catching the distinct smell of gas, she turned all the dials off.

"If he thinks I'm going to blow myself up playing around with this stove, he's crazy," she muttered, and walked away.

Before she reached the bedroom, she heard a pickup drive into the yard. Remembering that Travis had left in it earlier, she walked to the front door. Through the wire mesh of the screen, she saw him step out of the cab and reach back inside. Two gift-wrapped packages were in his arms when he closed the door and walked toward the house. An overwhelming and eager curiosity made LaRaine push open the screen door for him.

"I can't make the oven work," were the words she greeted him with, but she had difficulty tearing her gaze from the packages he carried.

"I suspected you'd get yourself in some kind of difficulty," he replied, and walked past her to the kitchen. "Show me what you did."

LaRaine showed him. "I smelled gas, but I couldn't see any flame," she concluded.

"That's because you have to light it. It doesn't have a pilot that automatically lights the burners or the oven." He set the packages on the counter and reached for the wooden matches in a container near the stove. "I'll show you." LaRaine watched. When he had it going, Travis turned it off and handed her a match. "Now you do it."

It looked much easier when he had done it. Finally,

after more error than trial, LaRaine succeeded in starting it. Travis checked the roasting pan and the roast inside.

"Didn't you season it?" he asked.

"No, was I supposed to?"

Travis handed it to her. "Salt and pepper it," he ordered with exasperation. "And add some water, just enough to cover the bottom of the pan."

"I didn't know," LaRaine defended herself, and did as she was told.

When the roast was back in the heating oven, her gaze strayed to the packages on the counter. She couldn't help wondering who they were for.

"They're for you," said Travis, as if reading her mind.

Gasping in delight, LaRaine mentally took back some of the things she had thought about him when she discovered the cooking and dishwashing that the job for him entailed. She reached for the smallest package first, tearing off the bow and the paper. Opening the box, she stared at its contents, a beginner's book on how to cook. Her wide smile grew smaller.

"I don't have time to give you cooking lessons. You'll have to teach yourself," Travis told her.

Less than enthusiastically, she offered, "Thank you."

The second and larger package contained something called a crockpot, obviously for cooking. Neither present was LaRaine's idea of a gift.

"It's an electric slow cooker," Travis identified the utensil. "The saleswoman assured me it was impossible for anyone to ruin a meal cooked in that. There's a complete set of instructions with it and some recipes."

"It was thoughtful of you," she murmured.

"I'm just hoping for a decent meal and doing what I can to see that I get it," he stated, and walked to the door. "Don't forget to put the potatoes and the rest of the stuff in with the roast," he reminded her before he closed the door.

LaRaine stuck out her tongue at the retreating broad shoulders.

CHAPTER EIGHT

As far as LaRaine was concerned, the evening meal that night was such a success that it even surprised her. When Travis came in she had the table all set, complete with a relish tray with ingredients obtained from the refrigerator. At his suggestion and with his assistance, she opened a can of green beans and heated them in a pan on top of the stove. The roast, potatoes, carrots, and onions were cooked to perfection. With every bite LaRaine silently congratulated herself. Cooking was a snap!

Joe ate with them, but he added very little to the table conversation. LaRaine had the feeling that he was silently in awe of her, which was a tremendous boost to her ego. Only two things kept the meal from being flawless: she had forgotten the coffee and there was no dessert. Travis corrected both of those by making a pot of coffee and taking some ice cream from the freezer.

Cleaning up afterward, LaRaine concluded, was a tiresome, thankless chore, and the only one with which Travis didn't offer to help. While she washed and dried the dishes, he went into the living room and did paperwork at the old desk. Joe disappeared somewhere outside.

When she was done, LaRaine saturated her hands

with lotion, determined that she wasn't going to get dishpan hands. She stared with distaste at the prunelike wrinkling of her fingers and wiped the excess lotion from her hands. As she entered the living room, Travis was closing his books and returning them to a side drawer. He looked up when she walked in.

"All through?" he asked.

"Yes," she nodded, and tried not to think about the state her hands were in.

Uncoiling his long frame from the chair, Travis said, "So am I. Good night, LaRaine."

"You aren't leaving?" she protested. "It's early."

"Not by my standards." He wasn't swayed by her argument. "Good night."

The house was unbearably empty after he had gone. Night-time made the rooms even more dismal than they were in the daylight. There were all sorts of creaking and groaning sounds coming from different parts of the old and tired house. Strange night sounds from outside invaded the house. Something howled mournfully and LaRaine suspected it was a coyote.

It was too depressing sitting alone in the house with nothing to do but try to identify the weird sounds. She wasn't all that tired, but sleep was preferable to boredom.

In the bedroom, she changed into a lacy black nightgown and climbed into bed. Immediately she rolled into the dip in the center of the bed, becoming nearly lost in the hollow. The pillow was almost as hard as a rock. She pushed it with her fist, trying to make an indentation for her head. Between the lumpy mattress and the hard pillow, it seemed to take forever before she fell asleep.

As soon as she did, it seemed that something was trying to waken her. She refused to rise to full consciousness. A hand was shaking her shoulder and she tried to shrug it away.

Dimly she heard a voice say, "Come on. It's time to wake up."

"I'm sleeping," LaRaine muttered into the mattress.

"Not anymore, you're not," the voice denied. "Get up!"

When she didn't obey, she was rolled onto her back. She groaned and looked through the narrow slits of her lashes. Travis was sitting on the edge of the bed, looking disgustingly rested. Beyond him was the window and a pinkish gray light in the sky.

"It isn't even morning," she told him, and shut her eyes tightly. "I'm not getting up yet."

"Yes, you are." A large pair of hands slid under her arms to sit her up in the bed, then stayed there to keep her steady.

At first LaRaine tried to push him away, but it was like trying to push a wall. Her fingers felt the flexing muscles in his arms—living steel. Slowly raising her lashes, she changed her tactics. Linking her fingers behind his neck, she arched her back in a feline gesture of tiredness.

"Please, Travis, let me go back to sleep," she coaxed with a little-girl pout to her lips.

He studied their unpainted ripeness. With scant effort, he drew her toward him. Half-drugged with sleep, it took LaRaine a full second to guess his intention. By then his mouth was tasting her lips, parting them with arrogant mastery. She seemed enveloped in a cloud of the manly fragrance clinging to his smoothly shaven face. The kiss was a slow insidious seduction of her senses, catching her at a moment when she was vulnerable and unprepared.

The pressure of his mouth became demanding and she found herself answering it, returning the ardor, and thrilling to the dizzying wave of strange, wonderful feelings. She arched toward him, feeling her breasts brushing against the cotton material of his shirt, their peaks inflamed by his body heat.

His large hands glided downward to the sides of her rib cage, his thumbs barely touching the swelling upward curves of her breasts through the lacy material of her nightgown. LaRaine didn't understand this wild, crazy fire bursting through her veins, but it didn't seem important that she understand it.

Then his mouth was pulling away from hers. Unconsciously a mixed-up sigh came from her lips as she opened her eyes to look at him. Something smoldered in his eyes, and her heart skipped a few beats.

"Travis," she whispered his name, and tightened the linking of her fingers behind his neck to pull him back and show her again the magic of his kiss.

"Get out of bed." The hand that wasn't supporting her slapped her thigh.

Startled by the stinging slap, LaRaine loosened her grip. She couldn't hold onto him when he suddenly rose from the bed. She quickly braced herself with an arm to keep from falling backward. When she didn't immediately obey his orders, Travis reached out and flipped the covers off her feet.

"Come on. It's time to fix breakfast."

"At this hour?" LaRaine didn't want to think about food. Her gaze kept straying to his mouth, wondering how much of the devastation it had caused had been real and how much of it had been left over from dreams.

Unconsciously she obeyed him in spite of her protest, swinging her feet out of the bed and onto the floor. Travis waited for her as she slipped into the black lace robe lying at the foot of the bed.

"I'll show you how to make coffee before I go do my chores," he said. LaRaine followed him into the kitchen, shivering at the coolness of the floor beneath her bare feet. He took the coffee pot from its place on the counter top and carried it to the sink. "I'm only going to show you how to do this once, so pay attention."

He was lecturing her again, like a teacher with a pupil. Some of her radiant confusion dimmed under his sternness. LaRaine watched how much water he put in the pot and how many scoops of coffee in the basket.

"Do you know how to do it now?" Travis demanded, and she nodded affirmatively. His gaze raked her with unnerving thoroughness. The faintly condemning light in his dark eyes made LaRaine pull the front of her robe more fully together. "There's bacon and eggs in the refrigerator. If I were you, I'd get dressed before I started breakfast. Joe is young and becomes embarrassed easily."

The implication of his comment was that LaRaine was accustomed to parading around half-undressed in front of strange men. She bristled in anger at the unspoken accusation.

"I fully intend to get dressed." She was wide awake now. "You were the one who dragged me out of the bedroom to show me how to make coffee. It wasn't my idea. And the next time you want to wake me up, knock on the door."

"I did knock, but you didn't hear me," Travis replied evenly. "Remind me to bring you an alarm clock so there won't be a repeat of this morning."

It wasn't exactly that LaRaine didn't want a repeat of this morning as much as she didn't want him making those kinds of remarks about her. Before she could open her mouth to take back her hasty statement, Travis was walking out the back door.

Angered with herself as much as with him, LaRaine stalked back to the bedroom. Stripping out of her night clothes, she chose a pair of white slacks from the closet and a black, gray and white patterned blouse. She tied a matching sash around her waist and turned to the plain, square mirror above her dresser to begin applying her makeup. The overhead light provided the only illumination in the room, which slowed her down. She was only half-done when she heard the front door open and slam shut, and footsteps walked to the kitchen.

"Where's breakfast?" Travis called.

"I haven't fixed it yet!" LaRaine shouted back, frowning at the dimness of the light as she tried to see if she had applied too much dark shading to her cheeks.

"Why not?" The demand came from much closer to her bedroom.

"Because I haven't finished dressing," she explained impatiently.

"You haven't finished?" Travis echoed. "I left the house thirty minutes ago. What have you been doing all this time?" He appeared in the doorway, a dark frown creasing his forehead.

"This light is terrible." LaRaine gestured toward the covered bulb overhead. "I can barely see to put my makeup on."

Travis stared at the collection of jars, tubes, brushes, and eyeshadow palettes on her dresser. "What is this?" he pointed.

"Lipstick."

"And this?" He went down the line, making LaRaine identify each one. Bottles of moisturizer, cleansing cream and skin freshener he set to one side along with a tube of lipstick. With a sweep of his arm he cleared the top of the dresser, dumping all the rest of her cosmetics into the metal wastebasket on the floor.

"What are you doing?" LaRaine shrieked.

"All the makeup you need is on the dresser." His mouth was drawn in a ruthlessly straight line. "No more makeup, LaRaine. No more masks."

"You aren't throwing all that away!" She grabbed for the wastebasket he had picked up. "Do you have any idea how much money that represents? Besides, those cosmetics are mine."

"You can have them back when you leave here," Travis informed her coldly. "In the meantime you have no use for them. There isn't anyone around here that you need to primp and paint yourself up for. And I don't intend to wait an hour or longer for breakfast every morning.''

"Are you going to give them back to me?" LaRaine demanded. "I want them back, right now, this minute!"

"When you leave," he repeated.

"Then I'm leaving now."

"Go. I won't stop you." He shrugged.

"Very well, I will." LaRaine pivoted away and stopped. Where would she go? How would she get there? She still didn't have any money. Travis was still standing in the doorway, watching her, knowing all along that she would have to back down. "Damn you!" Her chin quivered as she issued her taut acknowledgement of surrender.

"Start breakfast," Travis ordered.

It was several seconds before LaRaine followed his departing figure. Travis waited in the kitchen to assist her with breakfast. Joe walked in as she forked the almost burnt bacon onto an absorbent paper towel. Without her makeup, LaRaine felt naked and self-conscious, exposed somehow.

IT WASN'T A SENSATION that she became used to during the next three days. At odd moments, she would touch the bareness of her cheek with her fingertips and rail at Travis's arrogantly presumptuous order. The majority of her time was taken up with her job. It was all so alien to her that LaRaine was constantly coming up against frustratingly simple obstacles.

She stared at the gooey mess in the bowl and read the recipe again. Travis had suggested a cake might be a nice change for dessert. The soupy glob in the bowl didn't look at all like a cake, but she had carefully followed the step-by-step directions in the cookbook.

A fan whirred to circulate the hot air, its noise competing with the radio on top of the refrigerator blaring out a popular tune. The loud music usually helped to drown out the silence of the house. In her present confusion, it was only irritating. Stalking over to the radio, LaRaine switched it off, throwing the room into unnerving silence. She brushed a straying wisp of black hair away from her cheek, unknowingly adding a streak of flour across her ivory skin.

A hammering knock rattled the front screen door. The unexpected sound startled her and she dropped the batter-laden spoon from her hand. Swearing softly beneath her breath, she picked up the spoon and mopped up the mess with a rag. The peremptory knock came again.

Absently wiping her hands on the material of her slacks, she hurried into the living room. At the front door she stopped abruptly, stunned to see Sam Hardesty standing outside. His expression mirrored similar shock.

Sam was the first to recover. "What are you doing here?"

LaRaine swallowed. "I...I live here." She lifted her head high. "If you want to speak to Travis, he said something about checking some irrigation pipes."

"I thought you went back to L.A.," he drawled, paying no attention to the information about Travis.

"I didn't." LaRaine wasn't about to explain to him why. He had enough to gloat about just knowing he'd cost her the movie part. "If you'll excuse me, I'm busy. Goodbye, Sam. I'll tell Travis you called." She walked away from the door, her legs trembling.

Uninvited, Sam walked in. "Are you living with Mc-Crea?"

LaRaine would have loved to claim that intimate relationship just to watch Sam's mouth drop open, but she remembered Travis's statement about how quickly gossip traveled in this small ranch community and his desire to avoid unfavorable gossip.

"Travis is a gentleman," she declared, not slackening her steps to the kitchen. "He sleeps in the... bunkhouse." That sounded better than the shed. "And I sleep in here." But she didn't deny that there was a relationship of some kind between them.

"Why? I mean, if he's not your lover, what are you doing here?" Sam walked into the kitchen. "Good lord! You're baking!" he laughed incredulously. "I don't believe it—a domestic LaRaine Evans!"

"Why is that so funny?" she demanded angrily, turning on him in temper.

He stared at her, his gaze running over her face. Confusion flickered in his eyes. LaRaine looked away, conscious that her face was bare and open.

"You look different," Sam commented, unable to identify the cause.

She lifted a hand to her face, almost protectively. Her sensitive fingertips felt the powdery streak of flour and she rubbed it away. She turned away, picking up the bowl of cake batter and dumping the contents into a greased pan. Temporarily she forgot the uncertainty as to whether or not she had mixed it correctly. Once it was spreading across the pan she couldn't very well spoon it back into the bowl.

Sam moved to the counter, his gaze inspecting her profile. "You aren't wearing makeup," he accused.

"Since when does a girl have to wear it all the time?" She heard the tremor in her voice.

"I don't think I've ever seen you without it," he remarked. "You're...you're beautiful." He seemed surprised. "What's come over you?"

"I don't know what you're talking about." LaRaine carried the cake pan to the oven and set it on the wire shelf.

"No makeup, baking a cake, and I'll bet you're taking care of the house and cooking meals, too," Sam listed.

"So what if I am?" she challenged, feeling somehow degraded by his statements.

"There's nothing wrong with it," he insisted. "I just can't see you being the little homemaker. Not the La-Raine Evans I know."

"There are a lot of things about LaRaine Evans that you don't know." There were even a few things that LaRaine was just beginning to discover about herself.

"Why? I mean—" But Sam didn't seem to know what he meant.

"Maybe I just got fed up with that whole artificial world you live in," she suggested. "Maybe I decided it was time to get back to the basics of life."

"My God, LaRaine, don't tell me you've fallen in love with this Utah rancher? Really in love with him?" he exclaimed in amazement.

"I never said that," LaRaine denied.

"It's the only thing that explains it. I've heard that love can work miracles, but I never believed it until now."

"Well, it isn't true. I'm just working here because it's what I want to do," she insisted vigorously. "There's sunshine and free air. Nobody's living on top of you."

"As I recall, you referred to this country as a desolate wasteland." Sam wasn't believing a word she was saying.

"People are entitled to change their minds. As a matter of fact, it's supposed to be a woman's prerogative." She gathered up the mixing bowls, spoons and measuring cups and carried them to the sink. "Did you want to leave a message for Travis or not?" she demanded, afraid of his questions and comments.

"No, I'll call this evening and speak to him myself," he said.

"Then would you please leave? I have lots of work to do." The stiff request was issued as she started to fill the sink with dishwater.

Sam hesitated, studying the rigid set of her carriage before he finally complied with her request. From then on, everything seemed to go wrong. LaRaine forgot the cake in the oven until she smelled the smoky scent of something burning. When she rescued it from the oven, it was blackened and hard. She couldn't tell whether she had mixed it correctly or not.

While preparing the evening meal, she forgot to put enough water on the potatoes and they boiled dry, scorching them. The vegetables suffered a similar fate, cooked to the point of toughness. The jelly salad hadn't completely set, so it was like thick soup. Only the meat loaf in the crockpot was edible.

Neither Travis nor Joe had made a single comment. If there had been a hint of criticism, LaRaine was sure she would have dumped the food in their laps. Joe had pounded the ketchup bottle over his potatoes to try to drown the scorched taste. LaRaine attacked her meat loaf with angry frustration, her silence almost hostile.

She remembered to tell Travis that Sam had stopped to see him and would be back this evening, but she didn't volunteer the remarks Sam had made at the change in her. She had passed the information on in a brittlely curt voice. Travis had simply nodded, but his gaze quietly inspected her. LaRaine guessed that he was wondering how much of her brooding anger was caused by Sam.

All of it was. His visit had reminded her how far down the ladder she had gone. She was a housekeeper, paid a pittance. People, especially men, had always waited on her, not the other way around. She hated Sam for putting her in this humiliating position by getting her fired. And she hated Travis for rubbing her nose in it and making her work for the money she needed like some common servant.

She was washing dishes in a frozen rage when Sam came. Travis spoke to him outside instead of inviting him into the house. It was almost worse not being able to overhear their conversation and know whether or not they were talking and laughing about her.

After Sam had left, Travis came back into the house. LaRaine was wiping the last of the silverware dry and jamming it in the drawer. She heard Travis walk into the kitchen, but she didn't look up.

"Well?" she said in icy challenge. "What did he say about me?"

"Sam?" The inflection of his voice made it a question.

"Of course Sam," LaRaine snapped.

"He didn't say anything about you. He came over to tell me that they'll be using my cattle in the next couple of days and wanted me to drive them over to the set," he explained.

"I see." Her answer was stiff, not believing him. She felt his alert gaze studying her every move and refused to meet it.

"Joe and I won't be here for lunch tomorrow. Since you won't have to fix a noon meal, I thought I'd suggest that you wash clothes tomorrow," said Travis.

"Suggest or order?" LaRaine retorted sarcastically.

He ignored that. "If you'll come with me a minute, I'll show you how to operate the washing machine."

For a rebellious moment she didn't budge. Wadding the dishtowel into a ball, she tossed it on the counter and turned to accompany Travis to the back porch, avoiding direct eye contact with him. Previously LaRaine had only ventured onto the porch en route to the bathroom, never bothering to notice the appliances in the small addition.

It wasn't a sleek, modern automatic washer that Travis led her to, but a big, cumbersome, old-fashioned wringer washing machine. Two gray metal tubs were standing on legs beside it. LaRaine stared at the contraptions with growing dismay and anger.

"I'm not going to use that thing," she rebelled, turning the fiery brilliance of her dark gaze on Travis. "You'll have to hire someone to wash your clothes."

"I have," he replied evenly. "You."

Before LaRaine could argue, he began explaining to her how to work the washer. He showed her how to hook up the hoses to the taps in the bathroom to fill the washer and rinse tubs and how to operate the wringer and move it to use with the rinse tubs. He explained how long to let the clothes agitate in the washer and how to get a garment through the clothes wringer.

Lastly he showed her where the clothespegs were, to hang the washing on the line out back. When Travis had finished, LaRaine was choked into silence by the bitterness of her fate and the futility of protest. She managed a nod to indicate that she understood his instructions.

Her first washday was a series of minor catastrophes. Clothes kept winding around the rollers of the wringer. She tore the fragile material of one of her expensive blouses trying to pull it free, and lost a fingernail in a tug of war with the gobbling cylinders over the fate of a hand towel.

Two pairs of her knit slacks and one knit top shrank in the hot water. Two other blouses were ruined when her red slacks faded. The only damage to the men's clothes was the blue cast to their white underwear where the blue jeans had faded.

Her back ached from lugging basket after basket of wet clothes out to the clothesline and stretching her arms over her head to hang the clothes on the wire. It all had to be repeated when the sun had dried the clothes. Frustrated and exhausted, LaRaine was in tears by the time she finished.

If either Travis or Joe noticed her puffy eyes at the supper table, they didn't comment on it. Nor did they mention the new color of their underwear. To LaRaine, their silence seemed to loudly condemn her for not knowing how to do something as simple as washing clothes. If Travis had said one cross word to her, LaRaine knew she would have burst into tears. He didn't, and she kept a fingerhold on her composure.

CHAPTER NINE

OVER THE NEXT THREE WEEKS, LaRaine fought a bitter war to learn how to keep house. It was more than just cooking and cleaning and washing. It was retraining herself to hang up clothes, to put things in their proper place when she was through with them, and to organize her time. Travis expected her to make lists of foodstuffs and supplies she needed and do the shopping, with his accompaniment. LaRaine never remembered to write down everything she needed.

After she had received her fourth paycheck, she felt she had earned every dime of the money. The problem was that she hadn't been able to save it all. Because of her ignorance in not knowing how to care for them, some of her clothes had been ruined. The rest she didn't want to risk ruining by wearing them while she scrubbed floors or did some other equally physical task. So she had taken some of her money to buy jeans and cotton blouses that would stand up under the abuse. Also she had bought magazines to fill the empty evenings with something to do. At her rate, LaRaine was convinced it would take forever to save enough money to leave.

Her life on the ranch had begun to form a pattern. Sundays were supposedly her days off, the same as they were for Joe, who went to church and spent the day with his family. But LaRaine had no place to go and no way to get there if she did. Which left her and Travis at the ranch alone. As far as LaRaine was concerned, she was left alone since she rarely saw Travis on Sundays, or on Monday evenings, either, which Joe also spent at his parents' home. It was the night set aside by his Mormon faith to be with his family.

With the breakfast dishes done, LaRaine went to clean the bathroom, and a glimpse of her reflection in the mirror drew a stare. What had happened to that glamorous woman? There was still something faintly regal about the lift of her head and the wing of her eyebrows, but her face looked as scrubbed and fresh as a country girl's. How long had it been since she'd had a facial and a manicure, LaRaine wondered. When had a stylist last touched a comb to her raven black hair?

In a burst of rebellion, she dumped the cleansers on the counter by the washbasin. She wasn't going to clean any stupid bathroom! She swept through the kitchen, hating the ugliness of the house and the emptiness of it. She needed to be around people, to be the center of attention and to be pampered and fussed over. There had been too many lonely hours in this wretched place for her to stay within its confines another minute.

She slammed out of the house, not stopping until she was in the center of the ranchyard. She looked for the pickup truck that was usually parked by the shed. It wasn't there. Travis was at the corral, saddling the buckskin tied to an outside rail. LaRaine crossed the ground in long, angry strides.

"I want to use the truck. Where is it?" she demanded.

"Joe has it." Travis tightened the cinch strap and began looping it around and through the ring.

She pressed her lips together for an angry second, then demanded, "When will he be back?"

"He went into town to pick up some grain for the horses. He had a few other errands to run, so I don't imagine he'll be back until after lunch. You won't have to bother about fixing him anything." He unhooked the stirrup from the saddle horn and let it drop. His gaze didn't stray to LaRaine once.

"Damn," she muttered under her breath. A gust of wind blew a cloud of hair across her face and she pushed it back impatiently.

"Why do you need the truck?" he asked. "Did you forget something at the store?"

"No. I've got to get out of that house!" she exploded in frustration. "I can't stand it in there another minute. I hate it!" One way or another, she was going to get away from it. "Saddle me a horse," she ordered.

Travis turned, resting an arm on the saddle. "Where are you planning to go?"

"Over to the movie set," she retorted. "I have to be around people. I've got to talk to someone before I die of boredom. I can't take this place any more—it's driving me crazy!"

"There isn't anybody there."

"Where?" LaRaine frowned. "At the movie set?"

"The last of the crew and equipment pulled out yesterday." His level gaze watched her reaction.

She breathed in sharply at the news and looked

away, her eyes smarting with tears. She would have been gone too if.... There was no use finishing that thought. She had been fired. She was marooned in this godforsaken wasteland. Despair wiped out her anger.

"I'm riding out to check the cattle on the west range," Travis said. "Would you like to come with me?"

Shimmering with tears of self-pity, her widened eyes looked at him, surprised by his invitation. "Yes," she agreed hesitantly, expecting him to take back his offer.

"You'd better get some boots on." His gaze flicked to her canvas shoes and indifferently back to her face. "And put a hat on or you'll end up with sunstroke."

"I will," she promised, and hurried toward the house.

She was escaping her prison. Excitement seared through her veins at the prospect of accompanying Travis, forgetting that in a sense, he was her warden. In her bedroom, she took off her shoes and tugged on her boots. Grabbing a flat-crowned hat, she dashed out of the front door.

In the yard, Travis was astride the buckskin holding the reins to the saddled bay. LaRaine faltered in her approach, not quite believing that Travis actually intended to let her ride the big bay horse.

"You said once that you wanted to ride him sometime," he reminded her, his mouth crooked in a half-smile. "Here's your chance." He held out the reins to her.

LaRaine didn't need a second invitation. The height of the big horse forced her to jump to reach the stirrup. Once her toe was in, she swung onto the saddle. The stirrups were adjusted to just the right length for her to ride comfortably.

"Ready?" Travis gave her a sidelong look.

"Yes." She flashed him a smile.

At the slight touch of her heel, the big bay strode out into a canter. The buckskin matched its pace and was loping alongside within seconds. LaRaine marveled at the quickness and agility of her mount, considering its size, as it skirted clumps of tall brush with weaving ease. Shaking back her hair, she let the warm wind blow over her face.

The ranch buildings were far behind them when the terrain roughened and they were forced to slow their horses. Flushed by the exhilaration of the long canter, LaRaine felt really alive for the first time in weeks. There was a sparkle to her dark eyes and a softness to her mouth. The need to talk was as intense as it had been.

"Thanks for asking me to come with you, Travis." She was sincere.

"We still have a long way to ride, and the same distance to cover going back. I only hope you feel the same way at the end of the ride." But he smiled lazily when he voiced his doubt.

"I'm not worrying about getting stiff and sore." LaRaine shook her head. "I'm bound to be in condition after all the work I've done these last few weeks."

Travis took the lead up a rock-strewn ridge. As the sun marched higher in the dust-blue sky, the air became heavy with the pungent smell of sage. The broken valley floor sprawled for endless miles, gouged by dry water beds and mounded with small hills. Against the horizon was the backbone of a mountain range, a chipped peak standing out from the rest.

"I've never seen such empty land," LaRaine commented as Travis slowed the buckskin to a walk and her mount moved forward to walk beside him.

"It's part of the Great Basin of Utah," he explained. "Thousands of years ago, this was all part of a big inland sea that covered a third of Utah. The Great Salt Lake and Sevier Lake are the salt water remnants of it. A lot of people passed through here on their way to California and Oregon, but the Mormons were the first to settle. They called the land Deseret. It was proposed as the name of the state when it was admitted into the union, but Utah was chosen instead."

"What does that mean?"

"I believe it's from the Book of Mormon or the Old Testament. It means 'land of the honeybees.' The beehive is still the state symbol." He shifted into a more comfortable position in the saddle, the leather squeaking at his movement. "You've seen the highway sign in Delta, haven't you? The one referring to the Fort Deseret historical site. It's the remains of an old fort constructed of adobe and straw, built in eighteen short days to protect the local settlers from Indian raids."

"I remember the sign." She nodded, and looked around at the sprawling emptiness. "I can't imagine why the settlers would ever have wanted to fight the Indians over this land."

"Don't let the rock hounds hear you say that," Travis smiled dryly.

"Why?" LaRaine eyed him curiously.

"Topaz Mountain is to the north of here. They say

it's covered with deposits of topaz, amber and other gemstones.'' He studied the land they rode through. ''This country has a beauty all its own. It doesn't stun the eye like the splendor of the Rocky Mountains. It's more subtle—slower to make an impression.''

Her gaze swept the wild, rough landscape, sensing its lasting endurance in the tenacious sage and grasses. The gnarled and twisted junipers and piñon pines grew in spite of the aridity of the climate. She came close to understanding what he meant.

''You may be right,'' she conceded, but not whole-heartedly.

''Hold it!'' Travis reined in his horse and signaled her to do the same. He was looking to his right, his gaze narrowed alertly. ''I wasn't sure we'd catch sight of them,'' he murmured, a satisfied curve to his mouth.

''Catch sight of what?'' She tried to look around him.

''There's a band of mustangs.'' He turned the buck-skin and walked it slowly forward. ''We won't be able to get very close.''

LaRaine could just make out the shapes of grazing horses blending against the backdrop of a brush-covered hill. When they were a hundred yards closer she could see them more clearly.

''We'd better stop here,'' Travis suggested.

''I've never seen a wild horse before,'' she whispered.

''They aren't wild in the true sense of the word, not like the deer and buffalo,'' he explained. ''All of these horses are descended from domestic stock, so they're feral—they've gone wild.''

"They aren't as big as I thought they would be." Of the eight horses LaRaine counted, none of them was larger than a good-sized pony.

"The desert environment has bred them down to a size that can survive in this land." Travis pointed to a knoll near the grazing horses. "There's the stallion."

La Raine spotted the mustang instantly. It was poised in alert stance and seemed to be looking directly at them and testing the air for their scent. In the flash of a second the stallion was charging down the hill, neighing an order to his mares. There was a flurry of whirling horses and drumming hooves. Then they had vanished, racing over the hill, manes and tails flying. It took her breath away, the disappointment in their diminutive stature overridden by their wild dash from the threat of man.

"That was a sight to see," she breathed. "They're protected by law, aren't they?"

"Yes. It saved the mustang from extinction. The problem now is that the government has to come up with a way to control the mustang population the way they do with the deer and the buffalo. At the moment they roam pretty much where they please, mostly on federal lands leased by ranchers to graze their cattle. So there's an ongoing controversy between the rancher and the mustang supporters. Someday they'll find a compromise." He reined the buckskin around to resume their previous course. "Shall we move on?"

LaRaine followed—the image of the fleeting mustangs not leaving her mind. They rode in silence for a long time. The red, curling hides of Hereford cattle began to dot the brush, their white faces lowered to the ground to tear at the grasses amidst the sage.

"I want to check the water hole," said Travis, pointing to the left.

In unison, they veered to the left. A bawling calf greeted them as they reached the water hole, shaded by a small stand of cottonwoods. The upper half of the water hole had become a mud bog. The calf was up to its belly in the center of the bog. It made a puny attempt to struggle free when they rode up.

"He's stuck!" LaRaine cast a concerned look at Travis.

He was already shaking out his coiled lariat. Swinging it once over his head, he snaked it out to let the noose settle accurately over the calf's head. Taking a wrap around the saddle horn, he tightened the rope and turned the buckskin away from the water hole. The rope stetched taut as he began walking away. The calf bawled and struggled against the pressure pulling it to dry ground.

"You're choking it!" LaRaine cried in protest.

But Travis steadily kept his horse walking, pulling the calf through the mud. The calf's eyes were ringed with white. Determined to rescue the calf from Travis's abuse, LaRaine dismounted and grabbed for the rope.

"Stop it!" she ordered. "You're hurting it!"

Pulling against Travis, she tried to give the calf some slack so it could breathe. It was almost to solid ground; she could see it begin to gain footing. Ignoring Travis, she reached out to take the noose off the calf's head. At the same instant, its feet touched hard ground and it panicked, bolting forward into LaRaine before she could move out of the way. She stumbled backward, into the edge of the bog, lost her footing and sat down with a gurgling plop; mud oozed everywhere.

After an initial cry of surprise, she sat in shock. She lifted one mud-covered hand, then the other, and tried to shake her fingers free of the clinging webs of mud. The low, rolling sound of Travis's laughter didn't lessen the rise of her temper.

"This is all your fault!" she hurled angrily. "I wouldn't be in this mess if you hadn't almost killed that calf! I was trying to save it!"

Travis had dismounted and walked to the edge of the mud. He made absolutely no attempt to disguise his amusement over LaRaine's predicament.

"Look at me!" she demanded. "Just look at me! I'm covered with mud!"

She tried to stand up, but she couldn't seem to get her legs underneath her. Her boots kept slipping in the mud. Finally she had to put a hand back in the oozing slime for balance.

"Mud never hurt anybody," Travis declared.

As she was about to stand up, LaRaine felt a boot against her backside a second before it sent her sprawling forward. She screamed. Only her outstretched arms saved her from getting a faceful of mud, but the rest of her, from chest to toe, was packed with it. When she finally gained her footing she was in a quaking rage. The breadth of his shoulders was shaking with contained laughter. Her feet were weighted down with mud as she dragged herself free of the bog.

"You'll pay for that!" She stalked forward to confront him and carry out her threat.

"Why are you angry?" Travis mocked. "I've heard that rich women make special trips to beauty spas for mud baths. You got yours for free."

LaRaine swung at him, but he ducked and caught her arm. She lost her balance and fell against him, covering his shirt front with her mud. Automatically he circled a supporting arm around her waist, coating his hand and sleeve with mud clinging to her. As she struck at him with her free hand, Travis dodged the blow aimed at his head, causing it to glance off his shoulder.

Before she could hit at him again, his mouth was swooping down to capture her lips. Stilled by his sudden kiss, LaRaine was momentarily rigid in the iron circle of his arms. The searing fire of his mouth melted her against him, surrendering her to the persuasive pressure he applied. From blinding hate, she went to blazing passion. Primitive tremors quaked through her, bringing an urgency to her response that was more than matched by the devouring hunger of his bruising kiss.

His hands slid intimately over her body, finding the soft curves beneath their layer of mud. Their touch ignited more fires until she was burning out of control. Her senses seemed to explode with the heat Travis generated. She shaped herself to the hard contours of his length, glorying in the need he echoed. His mouth began exploring her face with rough kisses, sending shivers of delight down her spine when he nibbled at her ear.

Their desires had flamed into one fire until the downward path of his mouth encountered the mud-covered skin at her throat. Travis lifted his head, wiping mud from his chin and lips with the back of his hand. His dark gaze smoldered over her face as she slowly opened her eyes to look at him. She was weak with wanting him, but the sight of his mud-streaked face made her smile.

"You look funny," she told him, and lifted her hand to wipe the smear from his face, forgetting that her hand was covered with mud. A wider patch of brown covered his jaw. "Oh!" When she realized what she'd done, LaRaine drew her hand back, covering her mouth to hold back a laugh.

Travis immediately chuckled at the mud on her lips. "We're a pair now," he declared, and LaRaine found herself laughing.

She shook her head in disbelief. "I'm almost covered with mud from head to toe. Why am I so happy?" she asked.

"I don't know," said Travis, but the look in his eye was creating the most wonderful disturbance inside her. "But it's going to be a long, muddy ride back to the ranch...for both of us."

"Yes," LaRaine sighed, and reluctantly unwound her arms from around him.

Travis walked her to the bay and helped her into the saddle when her boot kept slipping out of the stirrup. His hand rested for a tantalizing moment on her mud-covered thigh. LaRaine thought he was going to say something when their eyes locked for a breathless second.

"Ready?" was all he asked.

"Yes," she nodded, holding the reins in her mud-slick fingers.

When Travis had mounted, they cantered their

horses away from the water hole toward the ranch. It was the most uncomfortable ride LaRaine had ever had, but her heart was singing all the way.

When they rode up to the barn, Travis said, "You'd better go and shower. I'll take care of the horses."

LaRaine glanced at his muddied front. "What about you?"

"I can get by with water from the kitchen sink and clean clothes," he told her.

Entering the house through the back door, LaRaine undressed on the porch rather than track mud through the house to the bedroom. She went directly into the bathroom, turned on the shower, and stepped under its spray. She heard Travis come into the kitchen and the water pressure faded when he turned on the sink taps.

Cleaned of the mud, LaRained turned off the shower and stepped out to towel dry. She was humming to herself as she slipped into the gold velour robe hanging on the door hook and zipped up the front of it. Her reflection in the mirror looked aglow with some hidden secret, but she didn't stop to delve into the mysteries of her emotions. She hurried into the kitchen to join Travis.

At the sight of him, she stopped. Bare-chested, he stood at the sink, bronze muscles rippling as he wiped his hard flesh with a towel. The desire she had known when he held her rekindled, the surging need threatening to buckle her knees. The silence of her bare footed entrance had not warned him of her presence in the room. When Travis turned to reach for the clean shirt draped across a chair back, he saw her, and the almost physical touch of his gaze sent her heart leaping into her throat.

"Hello, Rainey." His low voice was as caressing as his look.

LaRaine blinked. "What did you call me?"

Travis paused, as if unaware he had shortened her name. "Rainey." He picked up his shirt and put it on. "LaRaine doesn't seem to fit you anymore. Do you mind?"

"No." There was a breathlessness to her answer. "It's just that. . . I've never had a nickname before."

"You haven't?" One brow arched.

"No, at least none that anybody ever called me to my face!" She laughed a trifle self-consciously and looked away.

Travis had two buttons of his shirt fastened when he stopped to walk across the room to where she stood. He crooked a finger under her chin to lift it and let his gaze run over her face. Elemental needs throbbed between them.

"Travis," she whispered achingly.

In the next second she was caught up in his arms to be crushed against his chest. His mouth opened moistly over hers, taking in the softness of her lips in a devouring kiss. LaRaine arched on tiptoes, her hands sliding inside his shirt to freely explore the hard-muscled flesh of his chest and shoulders.

Her lips parted to permit the full passion of his possessive kiss to claim her. His roaming hands felt the bareness of her skin beneath the robe and sought the same liberties she had. LaRaine trembled as his fingers found the metal clasp of the zipper and her pulse flamed at its release and the first exploring caresses of his hands. She felt she would die with the incredible joy of it.

His mouth burned across her skin to the sensitive hollow of her throat. The loose robe slipped off one shoulder and Travis sensually bit at the ivory perfection it exposed. Her breasts throbbed under his expert massage, their rosy peaks hardened into erotic nubs. Seemingly with one hand at her waist, Travis lifted her feet off the ground, then with a half-muffled groan, he let her slide down until his mouth found her cheek and the lobe of an ear.

"You almost make me forget, Rainey," he murmured thickly.

It took her a full second to realize what Travis meant. She almost made him forget that woman called Natalie. Suddenly there was a ghost between them, summoned by his voice. The hands that had been clinging to him now strained to elude his embrace. The joy she had felt became pain. Travis overpowered this resistance, but LaRaine refused to be persuaded. At last he let her go.

Immediately she turned away, zipping up her robe with trembling fingers. It had almost been so beautiful. A tear slipped from her lashes and she hurriedly wiped it away.

"Gracious, it's lunch time!" Her voice quivered with the artificial remark. "I'll fix you a sandwich."

"Rainey, I didn't mean—" Travis began curtly.

In a flash of hurt feelings, she turned on him. "Yes, you did," she accused. "I'm not anybody's stand-in! I never have been and I never will be!"

A muscle flexed in his strong jaw. "I never said you were."

He hadn't needed to say it. Letting her gaze fall, she walked to the refrigerator. "I have some cold roast beef. Is that all right?"

There was a long silence before he answered. "That will be fine."

CHAPTER TEN

THE TAN AND WHITE PICKUP crested the rise and the familiar weathered-gray building came into sight. A kind of contentment drifted through LaRaine that they had finally arrived home after a long afternoon in Delta. The groceries were in the back of the truck, perishables stored in an ice chest. Most of the time had been spent waiting with Travis for a pump motor to be repaired.

Her gaze strayed to Travis. The wind blowing through the open window had ruffled the silver tufts above his ear and her fingers itched to smooth the hair into place. It seemed a liberty she was entitled to take after more than six weeks of almost living with the man. But her hands didn't leave her lap.

LaRaine hadn't forgotten that mud bath day—nor the crushing discovery that he thought of that Natalie person when he held her, nor the glorious ecstasy she felt in his embrace. There hadn't been a repeat of the incident. Joe had unknowingly acted as a deterrent on many occasions since.

During unguarded moments like these, she would look at him with all the intense longing she kept hidden. In a sense, they lived as intimately as man and wife. She cooked his meals, washed his clothes, cleaned his house, and went shopping in town with Travis at her side. But she wanted the pleasures that went with such a relationship.

The truck rolled to a stop in front of the house. "Home at last," Travis announced in a tired voice.

LaRaine pulled her gaze from him before he glanced at her. She didn't want him reading what was in her expression. Opening her door, she stepped down from the cab and her eyes focused on the house. Suddenly she was seeing it as she had for the first time, paint blistered away to expose the boards, a shabby old house.

Shock waves trembled through her. The sun must have begun to affect her brain! When they had driven up, had she really been wishing that she was married to Travis and this was her home? This pathetic excuse for a house? The man she married would have a mansion and servants. Had she lost her mind?

"What's the matter?" Travis questioned. "Did you forget something?"

"Yes." My sanity, LaRaine thought, then realized she'd given him an affirmative answer and took it back. "No, I didn't forget anything."

She walked to the rear of the pickup where the grocery bags were. Travis was lifting an ice chest out of the truck bed.

"Why don't you paint this place?" she accused. "It looks terrible."

"It does need it badly," he agreed. "I've got as far as buying the paint, but I haven't had time to do it."

"Take time," she retorted.

"When you're running a ranch, it doesn't work that

way, Rainey," Travis explained with amused patience, and carried the ice chest to the house.

Loading her arms with two bags of groceries, La-Raine followed him. He still used the shortened version of her name, and Joe, who was beginning to lose his shyness with her, had picked it up as well. Travis was in the kitchen unloading the perishables from the chest. LaRaine carried the bags to the counter.

"There are two more bags in the truck," she told him, and checked the roast in the crockpot. "Is Joe back yet?"

"He might be in the barn choring." Travis set the ice chest on the back porch. "I'll bring in the rest of the groceries."

The front screen door slammed behind him as La-Raine began unpacking the groceries. When one was empty she started on the next.

"Rainey?" Travis called to her from outside.

"What?" she shouted back her answer.

"Come here a minute."

She set the loaf of bread in her hand on the counter and walked into the living room. Through the wire mesh of the door, she could see Travis standing on the porch, looking off to the west. There seemed little reason for the urgency that had been in his voice.

"What is it?" She pushed the door open and stepped onto the porch.

He cast her a brief glance backward. "I want you to see this sunset."

"A sunset?" LaRaine frowned. "The sun goes down every day. One's just like all the rest." She turned to walk back in the house.

"Cynic!" he taunted, and caught her hand. "You haven't seen one like this sunset." He pulled her to the end of the porch. Placing both hands on her shoulders, he faced her toward the west. "Look at it."

The latent power of his hold tingled through her. He stood behind her, his body warmth touching the full length of her. Her pulse began behaving erratically, reacting to his nearness. She could feel the way his breath faintly stirred the top of her hair and caught the vague male fragrance of his shaving lotion.

Out of self-defense, she concentrated on the scene before her. The sun sank behind the far mountains, a blaze of orange red light fanning upward. A scattering of gray clouds was underlined with the reflected titian light and the valley floor was tinted with a yellow orange color.

"It is kind of spectacular, isn't it?" she admitted with awed amazement.

"Watch," Travis ordered quietly. "It will change."

It did. Like a slow-turning color wheel, the orange glare faded into a rosy pink, shading the clouds to a lavender hue. The fanning light of the setting sun began to fold up, leaving pale pink traces across the horizon.

A sigh of regret slipped from LaRaine's lips. Travis's fingers tightened on the soft flesh of her upper arms in silent agreement. The evening star winked from behind a wispy cloud tail. LaRaine lingered until she felt the provocative caress of his hands slowly and unconsciously rubbing a small area of her arms.

"Well?" he asked expectantly.

"It was beautiful." Her voice was tight, unnerved by the sensations running through her.

She turned, attempting to elude the excitement he was arousing, but Travis didn't move out of her way. Instead he smoothed a large hand over her cheek and lifted her head. The lazy smile on his firm mouth sent her heart tripping over itself.

"I'll make a country girl out of you yet," he murmured.

Her breath caught in her throat. At that moment he could have made anything out of her that he wished. LaRaine was putty, ready to submit to a master's hands, willing to please as long as he would go on looking at her like that. Then his gaze strayed from her and his hands came away as he released her completely from his touch.

"Hi, Joe," he said.

LaRaine took a shaky breath and glanced over her shoulder to see the young ranch hand walking from the barn. His hazel eyes darted from one to the other and LaRaine wondered how much he had seen. Her cheeks grew warm, and the faint blush made her angry.

Why was she embarrassed? She had done love scenes much more torrid than this in front of a camera with a multitude of people watching. The difference was that this time her partner in the scene was Travis. She bolted from that knowledge.

"I'd better see about dinner," she murmured as an excuse, and hurried from the porch before Joe reached it.

THREE MORNINGS LATER, LaRaine carried two of her blouses, that she had wisely learned had to be handwashed, out to hang on the clothesline. Travis and Joe had ridden out of the yard only minutes before. She had sent a Thermos of soup, some sandwiches and fruit with them since they weren't coming back for the noon meal.

With the blouses on the line, she started toward the house. She glared her dislike at the bare, grayed board siding. Then she remembered Travis's statement that he had bought the paint for the house. Pausing, she tried to visualize what it would look like with a coat of paint. It would be a distinct improvement, she decided. There was nothing wrong with the way the house was designed or built. It simply looked shabby and run-down.

If she had to live in the house for possibly another six weeks, why did it have to look as if it were about to fall on her head? She had become fairly organized in her housework. Travis might not have the time, but she could arrange to have it. After conquering the mysteries of housework, painting a house seemed remarkably easy to her.

With the decision thus formed, she went in search of the paint. She found the five-gallon pails in the storage side of the shed where Travis and Joe slept, as well as a small stepladder. She carted the stepladder to the house and had to drag the heavy can of paint. In the house, she rummaged through the junk drawer until she found a brush. Then, armed with all she needed, she began painting the front of the house, the thirsty boards drinking in the white liquid.

By the end of the day her arms ached from holding the brush. All she had painted was the lower half of the front of the house; the stepladder wasn't high enough to reach the second story of the house. LaRaine stepped back to admire what she had done. Already she could see the graceful lines of the building peeping through.

Pressing a hand against her lower back, she arched her spine to ease the cramping muscles. Then at the sound of drumming hooves, a smile curved her mouth and she turned expectantly to greet Travis and Joe as they rode into the yard. Her smile deepened at their stunned looks.

"What the hell do you think you're doing?" Travis demanded, the big bay dancing beneath him.

"That's a foolish question," LaRaine laughed. "I'm painting the house. You may not have the time, but I do. And I'm tired of living in something that resembles a broken-down shack."

"So you propose to do it all by yourself?" he challenged.

She had expected him to be pleased by what she had done, not angry. After all, it was to his benefit. She wasn't even getting paid to do this.

"Yes, I plan to do it myself," she retorted with stinging swiftness. "All I need is a taller ladder to reach the second floor."

"There's one in the barn," Joe volunteered the information.

"Go and get it," Travis ordered. "We have a couple of hours of daylight left. Between the two of us, we should be able to get most of it done before it gets too dark to see." His gaze slashed to LaRaine. "You, get in the house and start dinner."

"I said I'd paint the house. You and Joe don't have to help me," she protested at the heavy-handed way he was taking over.

"Let's get this straight, Rainey." His dark eyes narrowed dangerously. "I'm not going to have you waltzing twenty feet off the ground with a paintbrush in your hand when you don't know one end of a ladder from the other. You'd fall and break your neck...and expect me to pick up the pieces. Get in the house as I told you." He reined the bay toward the barn, muttering to Joe, "Like it or not we've got a house to paint!"

Subdued by his reasoning more than his anger, LaRaine went into the house to finish the last of the preparations for the evening meal. The next day Travis relented and permitted her to help as long as she kept both feet on the ground. In two days, the three of them had completely finished the house.

The results were so outstanding that after Travis had ridden out the third morning, LaRaine tackled the low shed, painting the outside, washing the windows and wiping down the interior walls. It looked remarkably habitable when she had finished. That only left the barn—but Travis had threatened her with violence if she attempted it.

"But with the house and shed looking brand-new, the barn is an eyesore," LaRaine had protested.

"In another month, I'll have the spare time to rent a sprayer and paint it. Until then, leave it alone," he had warned.

Instead of being satisfied with the transformation of the exterior, LaRaine was depressed by the ugliness of the interior. She glared at the dreary gray tile on the lower half of the kitchen wall. This room was the worst of them all, and the one she had to spend the most time in.

Absently she picked at a loose gray square with her fingernail. The tile popped off onto the floor. The one beside was pried free just as easily. LaRaine set to work. A few tiles were more stubborn, but they couldn't resist the efforts of a screwdriver.

Three hours later, squares of tile lay on the floor near two walls. LaRaine was halfway through with the third when she heard footsteps on the porch followed by the opening of the screen door. It was Travis. She had learned to recognize his footsteps by now. She glanced around at the destruction she'd caused and braced herself for his reaction when he entered the kitchen.

Two strides into the room Travis came to an abrupt halt. His gaze made a slow, sweeping arc of the walls. When it came to a stop to meet LaRaine's wary look, his mouth was grim.

"You couldn't stand it, right?" The question was dry.

"Could you, if you were in here hour after hour?" she challenged.

"Do you think that yellow glue dried on the walls looks any better?" Travis countered.

"No," she admitted. " I thought if I couldn't chip it off, maybe I could sand it smooth so the walls could be painted."

"Not a chance," he denied. "If you want to paint the walls, they'll have to be replastered, and I'm not going to that expense."

"I'll try anyway. At least, I won't have to look at that ugly gray tile anymore."

LaRaine returned her attention to the stubborn

square of tile and hammered the point of the screw-driver under its edge. Her hand slipped, grazing her fingers against the roughness of the dried glue, snapping a fingernail. With a startled cry of alarm she dropped the screwdriver and held the finger of the broken nail, as if to comfort it for its loss.

"What did you do? Cut yourself?" Travis was at her side in an instant, reaching for her hand. "Let me see."

"I broke a fingernail," she wailed.

"You broke a—" His mouth snapped shut on the astounded exclamation. "Good God, Rainey, I thought you were hurt," he muttered.

"I was always so proud of my nails." Tears misted her eyes as she stared at her hands. "They were always so long and now . . . now look at them."

She spread her fingers out for Travis to see. Half the nails were broken or chipped, filed down to a short curve.

"Rainey, I'm sorry." He attempted to be sympathetic, but she heard the underlying amusement in his voice, as if it were a silly thing for her to be so upset about.

"No, you're not. You don't understand." She snatched her hands away and sniffed angrily at her tears. "Where is there a pair of nail clippers?"

In the bathroom she found some and proceeded to snip off the long fingernails that remained. Travis frowned, "You aren't cutting them all, are you?"

"They might as well match the rest," she announced.

He shook his head, his mouth quirking. "I don't understand you, Rainey. One minute you are crying because you broke a nail—next, you're cutting them all off."

"I never asked you to understand me." LaRaine brushed past him to return to the kitchen and resume her demolition of the gray tiles.

"Yes, but I want to," Travis argued calmly, and took the screwdriver from her hand when she picked it up.

Setting it on the counter, he grasped her shoulders and drew her toward him. Her hands came up to rest in mute resistance against his muscled chest. His heady nearness shook her senses.

"You aren't the same woman who came to work for me. You aren't pampered or spoiled anymore. You're still headstrong and determined to have your own way—" his gaze flickered to the havoc she had raised with the kitchen, to prove his point "—but you've changed."

"Have I?" was all LaRaine could think of to say.

"Two months ago would you have done this? Or painted a house?" He eyed her mockingly.

"No," she admitted in all honesty.

"You see?" A dark brow arched complacently.

His gaze shifted to her lips to see her answer. They parted tremulously, but LaRaine had lost her voice somewhere in the turmoil of her senses. The distance between their mouths was slowly shortened by Travis until it didn't exist at all. A warm, rushing tide surged through her as her fingers spread across his chest, feeling the heavy beat of his heart. His drugging kiss demanded a response. LaRaine, who had long been addicted, it seemed, to his brand of kisses, responded willingly.

Before passion could run away with either of them, Travis was lifting his head and enclosing her in his arms. Her head rested against the hard pillow of his chest and she could feel the point of his chin brushing the top of her hair.

"Instead of replastering the walls, I could panel the lower half of the room," he suggested. "How would that be?"

"That would be fine, if you were lucky enough to find any wood paneling to match the horrid color of the cabinets," LaRaine dryly qualified her agreement.

"No new cupboards, Rainey," Travis denied in a mock growl. "I have to go to town tomorrow. I'll see what I can find." Sliding a finger under her chin, he lifted it up. "Is that all right?"

If he had suggested gray tile, LaRaine felt she would have agreed. "Yes."

His hard kiss was much too brief. Then he handed her back the screwdriver. "I'll let you get back to your work so I can do mine."

It was several minutes after he had left the house before LaRaine turned the screwdriver back to pry off the tile. He was such a handsome brute. She knew she was dangerously close to falling in love for the first time in her life—if she weren't already in love with him.

LATE THE FOLLOWING AFTERNOON, she dashed out of the house to meet Travis when he returned from town. Sheets of wall paneling were in the rear of the truck.

"You've bought some!" she cried, as delighted as if he had brought her home a fur coat.

Travis slammed the truck door shut and walked to

the bed of the truck. "Yes, I found some paneling, but I'm not sure what you're going to say when you see it."

"Why?" LaRaine frowned. Then he lifted the top sheet and she knew. "Gray!" She stared at the light gray, wood-finished paneling in disbelief. The rich-looking birch wood was attractive—but gray?

"Yes, I know," he said dryly. "You've just got rid of the gray tile. But before you explode, let me show you what I have in mind."

He carried the paneling into the house and propped it against one wall. LaRaine followed, liking the richness of the light birch but skeptical that it would work.

"What are you going to do about the cabinets?" As attractive as the paneling was, it clashed badly with the cherry-wood stain of the kitchen cupboards.

"We'll paint them white and antique them with gray to match the paneling," Travis explained. "It will lighten the room."

The idea immediately ignited LaRaine's imagination. "And for color, we can paper the walls in a red, gingham-checked fabric with curtains to match. And you could do the table and chairs to match the cupboards. The floor could be recovered in large squares of black and white tile."

"I hadn't thought about the floor, but—" Travis hesitated "—I suppose we might as well go all the way."

"When can we start?" she breathed excitedly.

"Is tonight soon enough?" he asked with amusement. "I can only work at this in the evenings, Rainey. I can't take any more time away from the ranch work."

"I'll help," LaRaine promised.

When Joe learned of the project, he volunteered his

assistance. Except for the painting, the two men did most of the work. LaRaine held paneling sheets and spare nails and pasted the wallpaper for them to hang. It took a week's worth of nights before the kitchen was finished.

When it was done, LaRaine stared in amazement. She had never believed the room could look so stunning. Even the old black and white gas stove fitted in perfectly with the rich, cheery room.

"Well?" Travis challenged. "Do you like it?"

"Like it? I love it!" In a burst of spontaneity, she hugged him. Locking her arms behind him, she tipped her head back. "We should toast it with champagne or something. Do you like it?"

"I love it." He huskily repeated her answer.

A painful lump became lodged in her throat and she suddenly wished that Travis was referring to her instead of the kitchen. But his love was already given... to that girl named Natalie. Forcing out a breathless laugh, LaRaine glided away from him.

"We don't have champagne, but there is some coffee. Would you like a cup?" She walked to the kitchen counter.

"No," Travis refused. "It's late. I'd better be turning in."

Her first impulse was to object, but she stifled it. "You're right," she agreed. He walked toward the door. "Good night, Travis."

"Good night, Rainey."

CHAPTER ELEVEN

THE PACKAGES were almost heavier than LaRaine could carry. They were so bulky and cumbersome that she could barely see where she was going. She hurried down the sidewalk. She was supposed to have met Travis twenty minutes ago. She would have been on time, too, if she hadn't happened to glance in that fabric shop.

The truck was parked at the curb. LaRaine almost sighed in relief when she saw it, knowing she would at least be relieved of her burden. The driver's door opened and Travis stepped out.

"It's about time." He lifted the packages out of her arms and set them in the rear bed of the truck.

"I'm sorry I'm late," LaRaine apologized, her arms quivering from carrying the heavy load. She hurried around to the passenger door, aware that Travis was anxious to get back to the ranch.

"What did you spend your money on this time?" He slid behind the wheel and started the motor, casting a bemused glance her way.

"Oh, I didn't spend my money," she answered brightly. "I spent yours. You owe me seventy dollars." She took a slip of paper from her purse. "Here's the receipt. Just wait until you see what I bought!"

Travis frowned at the receipt but didn't take it. "What do you mean, you spent my money? Or maybe I should ask what did you buy?" As he turned the truck onto the street, his gaze pierced her for a lightning second.

"You know how tacky the living room looks now that we've fixed up the kitchen," LaRaine began, unable to check the thread of excitement running through her voice. "Well, I was walking by this fabric shop, and there was a table of remnants, all upholstery material. There was one large piece of velour material. It's blue and gray with a touch of black. It will look just perfect for the sofa. Plus, I found two pieces of fabric, each of them big enough to recover the chairs. One is blue and one is gray. I thought we could re-upholster the furniture, strip the wallpaper off the walls and paint them an oyster white, or maybe repaper them with a silver pattern paper. A gray carpet with maybe a few threads of black would be perfect on the floor."

"We aren't redecorating the living room, Rainey," he stated.

"It wouldn't be nearly as much work as the kitchen," she reminded him. "Besides, you already have the fabric for the furniture."

"No, you have it."

LaRaine suddenly realized that Travis meant what he was saying. "But I bought it for you," she argued.

"I never asked you to do it. If you spent seventy dollars for that material, that's your business. I'm not going to pay for it or reimburse you." The set of his iron jaw was as unyielding as his stand.

"But it's part of the money I've been saving to go back to California," LaRaine protested.

"You should have thought of that before you spent it," Travis answered without a trace of sympathy. "Now you'll have to return the material and ask for your money back."

"It was on sale. They don't make refunds on sale items," she told him in a stiff little voice.

"That's too bad. It looks like you're stuck with seventy dollars' worth of material, doesn't it?" There was something arrogant in the mocking look Travis gave her.

"That's cruel, Travis," LaRaine snapped.

"Don't blame me for your own impulsiveness," he said with infuriating calm.

"What is this? Another lesson?" she demanded bitterly.

"I guess it is," he admitted. "I gave in to you twice—painted the house and remodeled the kitchen—but this time you aren't going to get your way. Maybe you'll learn that you can't decide for me what I want or when."

"What am I supposed to do with the material? It's of no use to me." She sat close to the door, on the verge of sulking.

"I don't care. You can reupholster the living room furniture if you wish, but you won't get any help from me."

And she didn't. Travis didn't lift a finger to help her when she attempted to re-cover one of the chairs. Fortunately Joe came to her rescue. He didn't know any more about re-covering furniture than LaRaine did, but his mother was experienced at it, so Joe asked her for help. Pride made LaRaine insist that she do it herself with only instructions from Mrs. Benteen. She wanted to prove to Travis that she could do it.

The recliner was reupholstered in the blue fabric. The chair to the sofa was in the dove-gray color. And the sofa, LaRaine's maroon monster, was re-covered in the blue and gray patterned velour. When the three pieces were finished, she waited for a comment from Travis.

For an entire evening he didn't make a single reference to them. Finally LaRaine challenged him. "Well? Aren't you going to admit that it's an enormous improvement over those maroon monstrosities?"

"Definitely." His dark eyes danced with wicked laughter. "You did an excellent job, too."

"Thanks to Mrs. Benteen." LaRaine gave the credit where it was due. But that wasn't where her interest lay. "Naturally the furniture doesn't look as well as it will once the walls and ceiling are painted and something is done about the floor."

"True," he agreed, but went no further.

In exasperation, LaRaine sighed, "If you know that, why won't you let me tear that yellowed paper off the walls and paint them?"

"Why do you care what this place looks like?" Travis tilted his head to one side, studying her curiously. "You'll be leaving in a couple of weeks."

It was true. Two more paychecks and she would have almost the five hundred dollars saved. The discovery jolted through her. There wasn't a thing waiting for her in California. But LaRaine could think of a reason that would keep her here—Travis, if he'd ask her.

"I care because... it gives me something creative and challenging to do." She answered his question the best way she could under the circumstances.

"In that case, go ahead."

LaRaine blinked. She hadn't expected him to give in, certainly not without considerable arguing. "Do you mean it?"

"Yes, on condition that I paint the ceiling," he qualified.

Joe came into the house as Travis said the last. He glanced at LaRaine and smiled, "Did you talk him into painting the living room?"

"Well, I didn't exactly talk him into it," she admitted, still surprised by how easily Travis had given in when he had been so adamant before. "He just agreed."

"When do we start?" Joe asked.

"You don't have to help," LaRaine protested. "Travis is going to do the ceiling. I can paint the walls."

"I don't mind. In fact, I enjoy helping you two fix this place up," he insisted. "Besides, it isn't going to be easy getting this paper off the walls."

Since Travis didn't make an objection, LaRaine accepted Joe's offer to help. But she wondered if Travis had noticed the way Joe had linked them together. She wasn't the only one who was beginning to think she belonged there on a permanent basis. Why couldn't Travis? This wasn't the kind of life she wanted... was it? But that was ridiculous. Everything about her seemed to be undergoing a change, her values, her life-style and her ambitions.

Removing the old wallpaper proved the most difficult task in redecorating the living room. The painting was accomplished over the space of two days. For the time being, the floor would stay as it was until the carpeting could be selected and laid.

Even without the carpet, the room showed the promise of gentle country elegance that LaRaine had envisaged. She wandered about the room, running a trailing hand along the length of the sofa back. She stopped at the desk where Travis worked most evenings, sitting in its straight-backed chair. She glanced curiously through the papers stacked on top of it.

She wasn't consciously snooping. The action was prompted by a curiosity to know more about how the ranch was run than anything else. There was very little to do this afternoon until Travis and Joe returned. She was filling time.

Absently she opened a side drawer. It contained ledger books and canceled checks. Bookkeeping was something that she didn't understand. She closed the drawer and opened a second. In among the papers, a splash of color caught her eye and she took a closer look.

It was a Christmas card. How unusual! LaRaine thought. Why would Travis be saving a Christmas card? And why would he keep it in this drawer? She knew she should leave it where it was, but curiosity got the best of her.

Taking it out of the drawer, she opened it. The usual Christmas message was printed inside, and beneath it, one name leaped out from the others—Natalie. The muscles around her heart constricted in sharp pain. It hurt to breath. She read the rest of the names on the card. It was signed: "Merry Christmas! Colter, Natalie, Missy, Ricky, and Stephanie."

It was obvious that Colter was Natalie's husband. LaRaine supposed the other names were their children. Natalie was married, but it didn't necessarily mean she was married when Travis had known her. She could have chosen this Colter instead of Travis. Although why, LaRaine could never guess.

None of that was important anyway. Travis had kept the card—that was what mattered. He had kept the card because it was signed by Natalie, and despite the fact that it carried her husband and children's names. It hurt to know he loved Natalie that much.

Strangely there was none of the consuming, destroying jealousy she had known when other women had claimed the attention of previous men-friends. This time, when she really cared about the man, she felt a deep, abiding ache that no tears could assuage.

Footsteps clumped on the floorboards of the porch. Startled, LaRaine rose from the chair. She forgot the brightly colored card in her hand. When she remembered, there wasn't time to return it to the drawer before Travis walked in. She barely managed to hide it behind her back. Her guilty conscience made her wonder whether it was her furtive movement that had drawn his immediate attention or if he had been looking for her.

"Hi, Rainey." His half-smile seemed natural enough. "What are you doing?"

"Nothing," she rushed, enforcing the answer with a quick, negative shake of her head.

A quick brow lifted. "Nothing?" His gaze swept her, alert and inspecting. "It looks to me as if you're up to something." He seemed amused rather than suspicious.

The card behind her back was scorching LaRaine's fingers. Her breathing was quick and uneven, panic quivering through her nerve ends. She had to distract him. She didn't want him to discover she had been snooping through his papers, however unmaliciously.

"Don't be silly." Her denying laugh came out brittle.

"Now I'm convinced. What are you plotting, Rainey?" His attitude remained amused and indulgent. "There aren't that many rooms left in the house. Which one is next?"

"Actually—" his comment reminding LaRaine of what had been only a half-formed idea "—I was thinking about my bedroom."

"I thought so," Travis nodded.

"It isn't what you're thinking," she hurried.

"It isn't?" he questioned skeptically.

"No." LaRaine couldn't move away from the desk for fear Travis would notice the card she was trying to hide from him. "What I had in mind was turning the downstairs bedroom, my room, into a study."

"A study?" He leaned against the wall, crossing his arms and bending one knee to hook a heel over the arch of a boot.

Her hand ran nervously over the smooth wooden back of the chair. "Every man should have a place to

work in private. The bedroom would work perfectly."
She improvised as she went along. "We could panel the
walls, move your desk in there and build some shelves
so there'd be a place for your husbandry books."

"It would give me a chance to spread out a bit and
keep down the clutter," Travis admitted.

"We could even put in an outside door. It could be
your ranch office as well as your study. You could con-
duct business from there. People, the cattle buyers and
grain sellers and other people you deal with, could
come there to meet with you," she elaborated.

"You make it sound as if there are people coming
and going all the time," he said dryly.

"Maybe not now, but in time I'm sure they will. I've
listened to you and Joe talk at the table. You've made a
lot of improvements on this ranch since you bought
it—drilled more wells and acquired more grazing
leases," LaRaine remembered. "I've listened to you
and Joe discussing the possibilities of putting more
land under irrigation to raise more hay and other
crops."

"My, my, what big ears you have!" Travis drawled.

"If you didn't want me to know, you shouldn't have
talked about it in front of me," she defended herself.
"You can't deny that you're ambitious. You intend to
eventually make this ranch the biggest and best
around."

"It isn't going to happen overnight. It's going to
take years and a lot of hard work." His gaze became
aloof and thoughtful, measuring her in a way that
disturbed her.

"I realize that." She gave him a wide-eyed look of

innocence. "What do you think of my idea about changing the bedroom into a study? There are three empty bedrooms upstairs, so it isn't as if there's a shortage of places to sleep."

"It sounds like a practical idea." Travis straightened from the wall. "I'm just curious about whose future you're planning."

"I don't know what you mean." Her fingers trembled around the Christmas card. "I'm not planning anyone's future."

"Aren't you?" Travis moved toward her.

LaRaine wanted to retreat, but the wall was only two feet behind her. She didn't dare turn or he'd see the card.

"If I'm planning any future, it's for the house," she insisted.

"What about yours? You haven't any thought in your mind about yourself?" He was towering in front of her, only a corner of the chair separating them.

"Me?" she laughed nervously. "I don't know what you're talking about. I'm going to California in a couple of weeks—or had you forgotten? What could turning the bedroom into a study have to do with me?"

Travis took off his stetson and set it on the desktop. "Are you leaving?"

Not if you don't want me to—but LaRaine couldn't say that. "Do you think you'll miss me?"

"Yes." Without elaboration.

"I'll miss you and this place," she admitted, then pulled a wry smile. "Although I won't miss washing dishes!"

She instantly wished she hadn't added the last. It had

drawn his gaze to her hand on the chairback, and instantly noticed the absence of her other hand.

"What have you got behind your back?" He asked the question in simple curiosity, but when LaRaine stiffened guiltily and the color washed from her face, his eyes became hard with suspicion. "What are you trying to hide from me?" he demanded.

"Nothing." Denying it was the worst thing she could have done.

"I want to know what it is, Rainey."

"Travis, no," she protested.

With calm deliberation, he pushed the chair up to the desk, eliminating the one obstacle in his path to her. As he moved forward, LaRaine backed up until the wall stopped her. She was trapped with no escape. Her heart hammered against her ribs.

"Show it to me." Travis stood before her, challenging in that quietly dangerous way.

"No." Her dark eyes implored him not to force the issue, but he ignored their plea. She pressed herself tightly against the wall, protectively shielding the card with her body.

Firmly, without roughness, Travis grasped her waist and pulled her away from the wall. She struggled frantically, but he simply overpowered her. Reaching behind her, he imprisoned her wrist and twisted her arm to the front. When he saw the colorful Christmas card her guilty fingers held, LaRaine felt his muscles bunch in silent rage. She flinched under his harshly accusing eyes.

"What are you doing with this?" he demanded savagely.

"I . . . I found it," she whispered.

"You've been going through my desk." The condemnation was swift and cold, shivering over her skin in icy chills. He ripped the card from her hand and let her go. "What were you looking for? My bank statements? I'm sorry, but you were in the wrong drawer. They're here." He snapped open a drawer to show her where they were.

"I wasn't snooping, Travis, I swear." Her voice broke and she tried to steady it. "I was just curious."

"What were you trying to find out? How much I was worth?" he snarled over his shoulder, his mouth thin with contempt.

"No," LaRaine denied quickly. "It never even occurred to me. It's the truth. I don't even know why I was looking through the drawers."

"It was just idle curiosity, I suppose," he taunted.

"Yes, that's all it was," she insisted. "I didn't touch a thing." Her gaze fell on the Christmas card his whitened fingers held. "Not until I saw that card, anyway. I couldn't imagine why you were saving a Christmas card. Then when I opened it and saw Natalie's name I . . . I knew."

Travis stared at the card, his expression unbelievably grim. In a display of suppressed violence he tossed it in the wastebasket. The involuntary gasp of surprise from LaRaine drew his pinning gaze.

"There isn't any reason to keep it anymore," he snapped, and raked a hand through his hair, rumpling its thickness.

"Colter is her husband?" LaRaine gave the statement the inflection of a question.

"Yes." A one word answer that raised more questions.

"Did she...jilt you to marry him?" she asked hesitantly.

Travis tipped his head back, a mirthless chuckle coming from his throat. "You've been aching to know the whole sordid story for months, haven't you?"

LaRaine swallowed. The crazy thing was she didn't want to know about it, not anymore. There was already too much pain. But Travis took her silence as a positive response.

"I worked for Colter." Travis held her gaze, refusing to let her look away. "I was his ranch foreman for more years than I care to remember. I met Natalie for the first time after Colter had married her. In the beginning she wasn't happy there, but then Colter's home was never a happy place. She wasn't there long before I realized I was falling in love with her." His voice seemed devoid of emotion. "I should have left then, but I couldn't as long as I thought she might need me. When I realized she didn't—well, it was a toss-up as to whether I was fired or quit." His mouth quirked in a cynical smile. "That's the story. Are you satisifed?"

"No," she muttered.

"Sorry I couldn't fill you in on all the details of our affair, but there weren't any," Travis said flatly.

"And the other names on the card are their children?" LaRaine felt stiff and brittle, an eggshell with a hammer poised above it.

"Missy is Colter's daughter from his first marriage. Ricky is Natalie's nephew. Stephanie...is their daughter."

"Travis, I'm sorry." Her heart ached for him.

"Are you, Rainey?" he challenged, a brow lifting in mockery. "I'm not."

Her throat worked convulsively as she turned away. "I don't know what to say."

"Neither do I." His voice sounded tight, heavy with impatient anger. "I thought you'd changed, but I was wrong."

"W-what?" LaRaine faltered in confusion.

"One of the few times that I don't bother to lock my desk, I find you going through it." The condemnation was there again.

"I told you I wasn't snooping," she protested again. "It was an accidental thing. I wasn't looking for that card."

"Would you like to see my financial statement?" Travis eyed her coldly.

"I don't care about money." LaRaine frowned.

"Outside of yourself, I thought money was your sole concern," he jeered.

"Maybe it was once," she admitted, "but—"

"—but not anymore." Travis finished the sentence for her. "You're no better at lying than you were at acting. You can plan on packing your things and leaving for California the day after tomorrow."

"But—"

"I'll give you the balance of whatever money you need." His offer stung.

"I don't want you to give me money!"

"Consider it a going-away present," Travis stated. "You're used to accepting presents from men."

Grabbing up his hat, Travis moved toward the door,

his long strides gliding over the distance. When the screen door slammed shut behind him, LaRaine winced. The door was being slammed on her. Travis was paying her to leave. He didn't want her around anymore.

If he had given her money two months ago, she would have kissed him for it and gone merrily back to California. But now the only place she wanted to be was here, on this ranch with him. Travis didn't want her to stay. He wanted her out of his house and out of his life.

Inside LaRaine was a frozen ball of pain. There was so much irony in the situation, but she found none of it humorous. There was no one to blame but herself. This was one lesson she hadn't counted on learning—how to hurt to the very marrow of her soul. She didn't feel bitter. The punishment seemed to be all that she deserved for the shallow and callous existence she had led before she met Travis.

CHAPTER TWELVE

ONE SUITCASE was packed and another was barely half-filled. LaRaine had been attempting to pack her clothes all day, but she kept finding excuses to postpone it. First she washed so all her clothes would be clean. In order to fill the loads, she had washed the men's laundry, too—at least that was the reason she used.

Naturally there had been meals to cook and dishes to clean afterward. The meals had been silent affairs with neither LaRaine nor Travis saying more than a handful of words. Joe had observed their frozen silence, but he seemed unaware of the cause, and unaware that La-Raine was leaving.

Convincing herself that she didn't want to leave the house dirty, LaRaine had throughly dusted each room. Now it was evening and she was alone in the house. There were no more excuses not to pack. She stared at the case sitting open on the chair. Sighing in resignation, she changed into the nightgown that she would wear to bed that night and laid out her clothes for the next morning, a practice she had only recently begun.

With that done, she began taking the folded clothes from her dresser drawer and laying them in the suitcase. As the suitcase slowly filled, so did the tears in her eyes until they welled over the dam of her lashes and began spilling down her cheeks. Her sniffling attempt to hold them back became hiccuping sobs.

Finally she gave up trying to check the flood and crumpled on the bed to bawl in earnest. She wasn't crying because she hadn't got her way or because her pride had been hurt. She cried because the one person she loved was sending her away. The lumpy bed shook with her sobs.

"Rainey?" Travis's haunting voice came to her, gentle with concern.

A hand touched her shoulder and she realized she hadn't imagined his voice. She rolled away from his touch with a start, her blurred gaze finding him sitting on the edge of the bed. His rugged features were drawn into a frown at the sight of her tear-washed face. She could imagine how terrible she looked with her eyes all swollen and red, and wisps of black hair clinging to her wet cheeks.

"What's the matter?" he questioned.

LaRaine turned her back to him and sat up. She didn't want him to see her like this. "Nothing." She choked out the word between sobs. She scrubbed at the tears with her hands, but more kept racing down to take their place.

"Why are you crying?" Travis wasn't put off by that lie.

"I'm not crying." LaRaine laughed a painful denial. "These are crocodile tears. Can't you tell?"

"No, I can't tell."

Iron fingers clasped her shoulders to turn her forcibly toward him. Her hands made a futile attempt to ward him off, but her efforts were pathetically weak.

She kept her face averted, burying her chin against her shoulder and letting the tousled black curtain of her hair fall forward in concealment. Travis was just as determined to see what she hid. When he attempted to push the hair away from her face, she tried to elude him and brush his hand away.

"Go away. Leave me alone," she pleaded.

Weaving his fingers into her hair, he cupped her head in his large hand and forced her face up to him. She kept her eyes tightly closed, but more tears squeezed through her lashes. Each time she breathed it was a sob.

"Those are real tears," Travis stated.

"Why are you here? What do you want?" LaRaine sobbed. Her shaking hands attempted to strain against the steel muscles of his arms.

"I knew you were packing, so I came to return your makeup," he explained. "I promised I'd give it back to you when you left."

"My makeup?" Laughter bubbled hysterically among her sobs. "My God, isn't that rich? I'd forgotten all about it!"

The hard shake Travis gave her stopped the laughter, but it also broke what little control LaRaine had on her tears. She no longer tried to fight out of his hold, but simply covered her face with her hands and began crying anew.

She didn't even make token resistance when Travis folded her in his arms and pressed her head against his chest. It was the one place in the world she wanted to be, whatever the reason. There was comfort and warmth and something strong and solid to lean on.

"Rainey, what's wrong?" Travis questioned in a low, soothing voice.

"Hold me, Travis. Please, just hold me," was all she asked.

He held her close and LaRaine buried her face in his shirt and cried. Her fingers curled into the material, holding onto him in case he let her go. His shirt absorbed the bulk of her salty tears.

When her crying at last began to abate into silent, sobbing breaths, she felt the gentle pressure of his mouth against her hair. She moved against it in a feline gesture that seeks the comforting touch. Travis repeated it near her temple, then brushed to her forehead and down to the damp lashes of her eyes. He kissed them dry and went on to her cheeks; he seemed intent on kissing away her hurt. LaRaine turned her face to receive his ministrations.

Soon her pain-dulled senses began to feel again. There was more than just comfort in the warm pressure of his mouth against her skin. It was a slow stimulating of her nerve ends, making them tingle with awareness. His hands were no longer simply holding her, but had begun a mobile and provocative exploration of her back and shoulders.

When his mouth moved near her lips, LaRaine moved her head the fraction of an inch necessary to intercept his path. Immediately his mouth hardened in possession, claiming the trembling softness he had previously avoided. She could taste the salty moistness of her own tears on his mouth. It only seemed to increase their thirst for each other.

Her hands crept around his neck, fingers sliding into

the sensuous thickness of his jet-black hair. The silk material of her nightgown made a slick surface for his hands to glide over in their searching and exciting caresses. Travis lifted her the rest of the way across his lap, crushing her to the upper half of his body.

The blue silk of her nightgown had twisted beneath her and ridden up. She could feel the roughness of his denim levis against the bareness of her thigh. The buttons of his shirt made a row of imprints on her middle.

His mouth worked over her lips, then moved to her ear, his warm breath igniting fiery responses. The bite of his teeth played with a lobe before he shifted his attention to the creamy curve of her neck. The nuzzling investigation turned her bones to water, waves of exquisite pleasure rushing through her.

The strap of her gown slipped from her shoulder. Tipping her head back, LaRaine gloried in the exploration of his mouth on her throat. The fresh, clean male smell of him, an intoxicating fragrance to senses that were already high, surrounded her. She seemed as high as the sun—bathed in golden light, afire with amber flames, and glorying in the magic.

Her fingers sought his face, trembling over the strength of his rugged features and drawing his head up so her lips could find the hard male shape of his mouth. The elemental hunger of its possession consumed her with its primitive needs until her heart was drumming to a pagan beat. Locked in a heated exchange of passion, LaRaine pressed lingering kisses over his face.

"Love me, Travis," she pleaded in a husky murmur. "Even if it's only for this one time."

"I will." Not letting her go, Travis began to lean

back, drawing her with him until they were lying side by side.

She had heard the rawness in his voice and knew he ached with the same needs she had. His hands slid across her stomach to cup the fullness of her breast. It seemed to swell beneath his touch with all the love she felt for him. To know his possession, she was willing to sacrifice her pride.

"It doesn't matter if you pretend I'm Natalie." She abandoned it completely. "Just love me, Travis."

His mouth bruised her lips, as if in punishment for raising a ghost. Just as roughly, it moved down her neck. The faint bristle of beard on his jaw scraped at her skin. A hand at her hip molded her more fully to his length, letting her feel all the hard muscles and taut desire.

"I can't hold you, Rainey, and pretend you're Natalie." Travis spoke against her skin.

Shivering from the rejection, LaRaine felt her hope dwindling. She had wanted him to show feeling when he made love to her, even if it was for someone else. She didn't want it to be just a physical thing, prompted by lust.

"When you're in my arms and I kiss you and touch you, all I feel is you." His voice seemed to vibrate over her skin. "I can't hold you and think of anyone else."

LaRaine breathed in sharply, then couldn't seem to release it. His large hand was sliding the drooping shoulder strap the rest of the way off her arm. The strong fingers running down her skin sent delicious goose bumps over her flesh.

"But Natalie—" She stopped, frightened of mis-understanding what he had meant.

Travis brought his attention back to her lips, his mouth teasing the parted softness. "You aren't standing in for her, Rainey." It sounded like a promise.

The bodice of her gown was pulled down, the opposite strap digging into her arm, and a caressing hand explored the exposed territory, climbing the white mountains to the rosy peaks. Its touch added to her disturbed excitement.

Wanting the same freedom of unrestricted touch that he had, LaRaine worked at the buttons of his shirt, loosening them until all were unfastened. His hard flesh burned with life. Curling, dark chest hairs tickled her palms, sensitive now as was every part of her.

One minute she was on fire in his embrace, but in the next, Travis was levering himself up to sit on the bed. Confused, LaRaine half rose, with an arm braced to hold her. She reached for his arm, wanting him beside her.

"Don't leave me, Travis." She was conscious of begging, but she didn't care.

His gaze burned over the rumpled cloud of her raven hair, down the kissed softness of her face to the half-fallen bodice of her nightgown. Slowly it returned to her beseeching dark eyes.

"I'm not leaving," he told her, and shrugged out of his shirt to toss it on her suitcase.

Then he was leaning back to her, his hand reaching out to slide off the one strap before he gathered her into his arms. The bared softness of her body was crushed to his naked torso, flesh meeting flesh and kindling one consuming flame. His embrace was unhurried as he kissed her eyes closed. Assured by his answer, LaRaine felt no need to rush, either, wishing to prolong the time in his arms.

"Why were you crying?" He nuzzled her ear. "You never did tell me."

He knew so much about her and soon would know so much more, there seemed no reason to hold back the truth. Vaguely, LaRaine was amazed that he hadn't guessed the reason. Her actions seemed to have made it so obvious.

"I don't want to leave tomorrow," she admitted.

"I thought you could hardly wait to get back to California." His teeth tugged at her lobe, his warm breath exciting her nerve ends.

She denied that. "I want to stay here."

"But for how long?" Travis muttered.

She intended to answer that, but the hard pressure of his mouth covered her lips and the long, stirring kiss made her forget what she was going to say. When it ended, she hadn't time to recover before Travis moved downward to kiss her breasts and she was lost in a whirl of golden sensations. Yellow fire licked through her veins at the intimate touch of his tongue. When he had her a shuddering mass of desire, he came back to toy with her lips.

"I love you." It was an unconscious release of the limitless joy that filled her heart.

His mouth became still for an instant. Lifting his head, he framed her face with his hands. There was a frowning look to his rugged features as his wary gaze ran over her expression.

"What did you say?" he demanded.

LaRaine wouldn't take it back, no matter what humiliation it might cost her. "I love you, Travis."

"Do you know what you're saying?" There was an angry tightness to his mouth.

Unable to meet the blackness of his eyes, LaRaine directed her gaze at the tanned column of his throat. It roamed over the breadth of his muscled shoulders to the springing mass of dark hair that wandered down his chest to the flatness of his hard stomach.

"I love you," she repeated. "I don't want to leave tomorrow. I want to stay here."

"A bird in the hand, is that it, Rainey?" The caustic sting in his taunt lifted her gaze to his compelling male force. "Have you decided that I might not be bad husband material after all since you don't have prospects in California?"

His doubt that she truly loved him hurt. The pain from the wound shimmered in her dark eyes. "I do love you, Travis." Her voice was small.

"Enough to give up the cocktail parties, jewelry and designer clothes?" He was skeptical. "There isn't any glamor here. Just hot sun, dust, and hard work. Is that what you want?"

"I've had glamor...and a certain amount of fame. It's pretty empty, Travis," LaRaine whispered, fighting the ache in her throat. "Look at my hands. I have stubby nails and even a couple of calluses. I know what I'm letting myself in for when I say I want to stay here."

"Do you, Rainey? My God, do you?" There was an almost desperate ring to his demand. His hands unconsciously tightened around her face, inflicting pain. "It might be years before I can afford to give you any of the luxuries you dream about."

"I don't want you to give me anything," she protested. "I only want to love you and help you and work with you to make this ranch the best in Utah. I know it's hard to believe, coming from me. I even find it strange, but deep down inside that's the way I really feel."

His taut muscles began to relax. "You haven't hated it here? All the hard work? The isolation?" he questioned further.

"It's been work, but I haven't hated it. In a way, I've kind of enjoyed it." Which was something she had been slow to admit to herself. LaRaine ran her hand lightly over his powerful shoulder. "Except at night. It was empty in this house all by myself." She looked at him, loving the vital, male face. "Would you sleep with me tonight, Travis, so it won't be so lonely in this bed?"

She could almost hear a silent chuckle in the warm breath he expelled. His mouth came down to lightly take her lips and nibble at their softness.

"If you thought it was lonely here—" his warm breath mingled with hers "—you should have tried sleeping in that shed! It was hell sleeping in that cot and imagining you in my bed."

"Did it really bother you?" she whispered.

"Bother me? You've bothered me since the day I saw you in that sultry pose when I rode up." Travis kissed her hard, driving her lips against the white barrier of her teeth. After a punishing minute, the pressure eased to a gentler level. "That's why I moved to the shed. I knew you wouldn't be sleeping in this bed alone if I stayed in the house."

"Really?" LaRaine drew back, wanting to see his face.

"Yes, really." A smile deepened the corners of his mouth.

"But...why?" She didn't understand.

"I'd already been burned once by falling in love with the wrong woman. I didn't want it to happen again. The problem was there wasn't a whole helluva lot I could do to prevent it," he told her.

"You mean...." She breathed in. "You said you loved Natalie? That I almost made you forget her?"

"In the beginning, it was true. But it didn't take me long to realize that when I kissed you, I wasn't thinking about Natalie." Travis kissed her again, as if to prove it, and it was a while before he let her up for air.

"Do you still love her?" LaRaine questioned. His hands had begun a series of arousing caresses. Soon she wouldn't care about his answer.

"Not in the same way I once did. I care about her, I admire her. If she needed my help tomorrow, I'd be there," Travis told her. "I felt gentle and protective toward her. With you, the love I feel is strong and fierce, something I can't control."

Rocked by his confession. LaRaine wound her arms around him, too happy to speak. When she attempted to hide her face in the curve of his neck, Travis lifted it to claim her lips in a branding kiss and she abandoned herself to the delights of his embrace and the persuasive ardor of his mouth. She placed herself in the hands of an expert and learned more lessons from him in the art of giving.

"We can drive to Nevada in the morning and be married in Ely," Travis told her. "Unless you want to go tonight." LaRaine trembled with the passion he had deliberately aroused.

Rubbing the roughness of his cheek against hers, he warned, "We won't have a honeymoon, Rainey. I can't spare the time away from the ranch."

Her fingers lovingly traced the chiseled outline of his face, so powerful and strong. "Do you think I care?" she whispered, then smiled. "Mrs. Travis McCrea isn't going to be able to spare the time, either."

When Travis lifted his head, her hand slid to his mouth to brush her fingertips over its hard, male shape. Before they could flutter away he caught them and kissed them individually. His eyes locked with hers.

"Rainey McCrea. That name will never light any theater marquee. Are you sorry?" he asked.

"Not a bit," she assured him. Personally she thought the name sounded magical. "I have something more wonderful than the make-believe world ever dreamed about. Why would I be sorry about that?"

"I only want you to be very sure," said Travis.

"Believe me, I am," LaRaine promised.

Travis rolled onto his back, pulling her on top of him. His hands covered her ribs, then moved to hold themselves to her breasts. Her nightgown slid down a little farther and a muscled thigh impeded its downward progress. Tucking the sides of her hair behind her ears, LaRaine leaned down to kiss him.

Eluding her for a moment, he asked, "Are you sure you want to turn this room into a study?"

Deprived of his mouth, LaRaine settled for the slashing indentation near it. "Why? Don't you?"

"It's a good idea," he agreed, a hand sliding around to the small of her back. "But I was thinking it would be nice if the child we conceive in this room could sleep here, too, until it's old enough to sleep alone upstairs."

"Child?" A thread of panic ran through her voice.

"Don't you want to have a family?" Travis kissed the lips he had been avoiding.

"I don't know," she murmured. "Travis, I don't know if I can take care of a baby. I've never held one in my life. What if I dropped it?"

"You won't," he chuckled. "What we'll have to do is experiment with the first one. Then depending on how quickly you learn, we can see about enlarging the family."

He made it sound so simple and uncomplicated. He truly believed she could cope with anything. And because he believed it, LaRaine did, too. The idea of holding a dark-haired, dark-eyed baby didn't seem quite as frightening. In fact, she felt a faint curling of excitement at the thought.

"Do you want a baby right away?" she asked.

"Nature decrees that there be a certain waiting period." Travis gently mocked her lack of knowledge about babies and their care. "I don't know about you, but I'm not getting any younger. I'd rather not wait too long before starting a family."

She touched the silver tufts that streaked the sides of his jet black hair. "You're just in your prime, Travis."

"You think so?" A wicked light danced in his eyes as his mouth slanted.

His strong arms held her as he shifted on the bed, turning them together until her shoulders were on the mattress and his crushing weight pressed her down. LaRaine only had a second to marvel at how easily her smaller frame fitted itself to the hard contours of his male length—the differences being one of the most glorious things. It was a passing discovery that was soon blotted out by the searing fire of his kiss. All her attention was devoted to learning the responses he wanted. When he had built her desire to a fever pitch of longing, she felt his weight ease.

"Travis, no!" Her fingers dug into the muscled flesh of his shoulders. "You aren't going to do the gentlemanly thing and sleep in the shed, are you?" she protested in a voice that revealed her ache.

"I told you once that I'm not a gentleman."

A boot hit the floor with a loud thud.

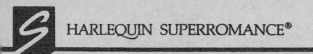
HARLEQUIN SUPERROMANCE®

A PLACE IN HER HEART ...

Somewhere deep in the heart of every grown woman is the little girl she used to be....

In September, October and November 1992, the world of childhood and the world of love collide in six very special romance titles. Follow these six special heroines as they discover the sometimes heart-wrenching, always heartwarming joy of being a Big Sister.

Written by six of your favorite Superromance authors, these compelling and emotionally satisfying romantic stories will earn a place in your heart!

SEPTEMBER 1992

#514   NOTHING BUT TROUBLE—Sandra James
#515   ONE TO ONE—Marisa Carroll

OCTOBER 1992

#518   OUT ON A LIMB—Sally Bradford
#519   STAR SONG—Sandra Canfield

NOVEMBER 1992

#522   JUST BETWEEN US—Debbi Bedford
#523   MAKE-BELIEVE—Emma Merritt

AVAILABLE WHEREVER HARLEQUIN SUPERROMANCE BOOKS ARE SOLD

WELCOME TO

The quintessential small town,
where everyone knows everybody else!

Each book set in Tyler is a self-contained love story; together,
the twelve novels stitch the fabric of the community.

"The small town warmth and friendliness shine through."
Rendezvous

Join your friends in Tyler for the tenth book,
CROSSROADS by Marisa Carroll, available in December.

*Can Dr. Jeffrey Baron and nurse Cecelia Hayes discover
what's killing the residents of Worthington House?*

GREAT READING...GREAT SAVINGS...AND A
FABULOUS FREE GIFT!

With Tyler you can receive a fabulous gift, ABSOLUTELY FREE,
by collecting proofs-of-purchase found in each Tyler book.
And use our special Tyler coupons to save on your next
TYLER book purchase.

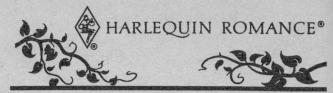

HARLEQUIN ROMANCE®

After her father's heart attack, Stephanie Bloomfield comes home to Orchard Valley, Oregon, to be with him and with her sisters.

Orchard Valley

Steffie learns that many things have changed in her absence—but not her feelings for journalist Charles Tomaselli. He was the reason she left Orchard Valley. Now, three years later, will he give her a reason to stay?

"The Orchard Valley trilogy features three delightful, spirited sisters and a trio of equally fascinating men. The stories are rich with the romance, warmth of heart and humor readers expect, and invariably receive, from Debbie Macomber."

—Linda Lael Miller

Don't miss the Orchard Valley trilogy by Debbie Macomber:

VALERIE   Harlequin Romance #3232 (November 1992)
STEPHANIE   Harlequin Romance #3239 (December 1992)
NORAH   Harlequin Romance #3244 (January 1993)

Look for the special cover flash on each book!

Available wherever Harlequin books are sold.

ORC-2

HARLEQUIN®

Temptation®

the **Fortune Boys**

A funny, sexy miniseries from bestselling
author Elise Title!

LOSING THEIR HEARTS MEANT
LOSING THEIR FORTUNES....

If any of the four Fortune brothers were unfortunate enough to
wed, they'd be permanently divorced from the Fortune
millions—thanks to their father's last will and testament.

BUT CUPID HAD OTHER PLANS!
Meet Adam in #412 **ADAM & EVE** (Sept. 1992)
Meet Peter #416 **FOR THE LOVE OF PETE**
(Oct. 1992)
Meet Truman in #420 **TRUE LOVE** (Nov. 1992)
Meet Taylor in #424 **TAYLOR MADE** (Dec. 1992)

WATCH THESE FOUR MEN TRY TO WIN
AT LOVE AND NOT FORFEIT $$$

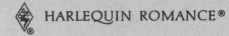